Jessica snuggled closer to Jonathan in the cave and entwined her arms around his neck. "I love you so much," she declared.

Jonathan faced front, staring into the distance. The flames of the fire illuminated the finely shaped features of his beautiful face. "I'm very different from the other guys you know," he whispered.

"I'll say you are!" she agreed enthusiastically.

Suddenly Jonathan jumped up and scrambled out of the cave. Jessica frowned, confused, as she watched him toss sand over their fire to put out the flames.

A moment later she heard what had startled him. Loud voices were coming from a short distance down the beach. Her mind snapped to attention, and a shiver of fear raced up and down her spine. "Oh, my gosh, what if it's the murderer?" she cried softly.

Jonathan crawled back into the cave and pulled her close. "I guarantee you," he whispered in her ear, "it's not the killer."

KISS OF A KILLER

Written by
Kate William

Created by
FRANCINE PASCAL

BANTAM BOOKS
NEW YORK · TORONTO · LONDON · SYDNEY · AUCKLAND

RL 6, age 12 and up

KISS OF A KILLER

A Bantam Book / November 1996

Sweet Valley High® is a registered trademark of Francine Pascal.
Conceived by Francine Pascal.
Produced by Daniel Weiss Associates, Inc.
33 West 17th Street
New York, NY 10011.
Cover art by Bruce Emmett.

ISBN: 0-553-57049-8

Published simultaneously in the United States and Canada

Bantam Books are published by Bantam Books, a division of Bantam
Doubleday Dell Publishing Group, Inc. Its trademark, consisting of the
words "Bantam Books" and the portrayal of a rooster, is Registered in U.S.
Patent and Trademark Office and in other countries. Marca Registrada.
Bantam Books, 1540 Broadway, New York, New York 10036.

PRINTED IN THE UNITED STATES OF AMERICA

OPM   0 9 8 7 6 5 4 3 2 1

To Anita Elliott Kaller

Chapter 1

Elizabeth Wakefield slowly opened her eyes and moaned as waves of dizziness crashed over her. The scent of burning candle wax lingered in the air, nagging her memory. Something sinister lurked in the back of her mind.

She was surprised to find herself snuggled in Todd Wilkins's arms, gazing into his coffee brown eyes. Behind him, the dimly lit living room was decorated with balloons and streamers. Everything seemed to be spinning in a kaleidoscope of muted colors and strange shadows. One sleeve of her long blue dress felt damp and sticky from someone's having dribbled fruit punch down her arm.

Elizabeth blinked, trying to untangle her jumbled thoughts. She knew she was at a party at the home of Jonathan Cain, a new student at Sweet

Valley High, whose crumbling old mansion was as weird and unsettling as he was.

Elizabeth also remembered that she'd come to keep an eye on her twin sister, Jessica, who had developed an outrageous crush on Jonathan. But beyond those sketchy facts, Elizabeth's thoughts were a blur.

Todd gently pushed a strand of long blond hair back from her face. "Are you OK?" he asked.

Elizabeth sighed, warmed by his tender concern. "I think so." Although she and Todd had recently broken off their longtime relationship, Elizabeth wished she could stay in his arms forever, safe and warm. "What happened?" she murmured.

"You fainted," he answered softly.

She nodded, then groaned as the room began to spin faster. *Fainted*, Elizabeth repeated silently. She tried to recall why she'd fainted, but her mind drew a blank. *It was something bad*, she thought uneasily. She realized she didn't want to remember.

The sound of Amy Sutton's anguished screams penetrated Elizabeth's foggy brain, bringing back the horror she'd tried to forget.

She closed her eyes as vivid memories flashed through her mind. The party had been in full swing, the room bathed in an eerie yellow light from all the candles the guys had set up earlier. Couples had been dancing to music provided by someone's CD player. Elizabeth remembered feeling miserable as she'd watched Todd slow-dancing with Amy's cousin Katrina.

All of a sudden a gust of wind had whipped through the room, blowing out the candles. At the very same moment the electricity had gone off, killing the music and the lights, plunging the room into darkness. Most of the group had cheered, but Elizabeth had been frantic with fear for her sister's safety.

Although the twins were identical, sharing the same silky blond hair, blue-green eyes, and lean, athletic build, their personalities were as different as if they'd come from two separate planets. Jessica, the younger twin by four minutes, had an adventurous streak as wide as the Grand Canyon. She rarely worried about the consequences of her actions—especially when she was in love.

Elizabeth, although born only four minutes before her twin, was very much the older sister—serious, studious, cautious, and responsible. Jessica seemed to get herself into one jam after another, and more often than not it was Elizabeth who came to her rescue.

When the lights had gone out, Elizabeth's mind flashed a warning that her twin was in danger. All she'd wanted to do was find Jessica and get out of Jonathan's spooky mansion.

Elizabeth and Todd had teamed up to look for a fuse box. After groping around in the dark for some time, they'd finally located it in the basement and managed to turn the lights back on.

But Elizabeth's relief had lasted only a few seconds. When she and Todd had returned to the living room, they'd found Katrina Sutton lying motionless on the floor with a horrible bite mark on her neck, her skin as white and waxy as the extinguished candles that circled the room.

In an upstairs bedroom of the mansion, Jessica felt as if she were floating on a heavenly cloud as she snuggled closer to Jonathan. The evening was turning out to be a dream come true.

Jonathan shifted his position on the bare mattress of the huge four-poster bed so that his face was directly above hers, his radiant blue eyes piercing hers like laser beams. Jessica's breath caught in her throat as he lowered his lips to hers for a deep, searing kiss that shot thrills up and down her spine.

Weeks earlier, the day Jonathan had first arrived at Sweet Valley High, Jessica had taken one look and immediately recognized him as her destiny. Although it had seemed as if every other girl in the school was also chasing him, Jessica never doubted that she and Jonathan belonged together.

But for some reason, Jonathan had avoided her in the beginning. With every step she'd taken toward him, he'd pushed her away. For a while Jonathan had even pretended to prefer Enid Rollins, Elizabeth's drippy best friend. But Jessica hadn't been fooled for long.

That night everything had changed. Jonathan had finally admitted that he loved her and wanted to be with her forever. *That's how long I want to stay right here in Jonathan's arms,* Jessica silently declared. *Forever.*

But slowly, screams coming from downstairs invaded her thoughts, like an alarm clock shattering a dream. Jessica wrinkled her nose and stirred. "What's going on?" she murmured.

Jonathan arched his eyebrows. "I haven't the faintest idea."

A crowd was gathered around Katrina, everyone gaping in frozen shock. *I have to do something,* Elizabeth thought urgently. With regret, she forced herself to leave the safe haven of Todd's arms.

"Someone call nine-one-one!" she screamed as she pushed her way through the crowd. Her take-charge tone finally sank in, and several bewildered faces turned to her. Lila Fowler, Jessica's and Amy's good friend, ran to the phone. The others stepped back to make room for Elizabeth. She dropped to her knees beside Katrina and began administering CPR.

Beads of sweat formed on Elizabeth's forehead, dripping into her eyes as she continued breathing into Katrina's mouth and pushing down on her chest.

At one point Elizabeth looked up, and her gaze fell on a portrait hanging over the fireplace. It was of a young man in a black eighteenth-century riding outfit. Something about the picture nagged at her for an instant. But she quickly turned back to her efforts to resuscitate Katrina, blocking everything out of her mind except the rhythm of CPR—*breathe in, breathe out, push—one, two, three, four, five.* . . .

Minutes passed, which seemed like hours, but Katrina wasn't responding. Her face remained deathly pale. Elizabeth's shoulders ached, but she refused to give up hope. She continued with renewed fervor. *You're going to make it, Katrina,* she vowed, pushing away any doubt of the girl's recovery.

Someone is going to be in big trouble, Jessica vowed as she and Jonathan stomped down the stairs. She expected to find a practical joke in progress or something equally ridiculous. After having waited so long to be with Jonathan, she wasn't in the mood for childish games. She fully intended to unleash her fury on the jerk whose

6

rotten timing had interrupted the most romantic moment of her life.

Jessica reached the landing and marched across the room where a crowd had gathered. She put her hands on her hips and pursed her lips. "What is the meaning of this?" she shouted. "Can't you guys—"

The rest of her words died in her throat as she looked around the room, noticing the shocked expression on everyone's face. Jessica gasped as she caught sight of Elizabeth kneeling over Katrina's lifeless body, breathing into her mouth.

This can't be happening, Jessica thought, raising her trembling hand to her lips. Standing near her cousin's body, Amy sobbed hysterically in Lila's arms. Jessica moved closer to them, and the three friends huddled together.

"What happened?" Jessica asked.

Amy shook her head, obviously too distraught to speak.

"No one knows," Lila answered in a small, shaky voice. "The lights went off, and when they finally came back on, Katrina was . . . like that." Lila gestured to where Katrina lay.

Amy began to cry louder.

Lila patted her friend's back, then turned to Jessica with a look of sheer terror. "This is horrible," Lila whispered, "worse than . . . that other time."

Jessica nodded gravely. "I know." She and Lila

had recently discovered a dead body drained of blood in a Dumpster outside the Dairi Burger, a popular hangout in Sweet Valley. Dean Maddingly, a seventeen-year-old from the nearby town of Big Mesa, had turned out to be the first local victim of a serial killer who police believed was still loose in Sweet Valley. A few weeks later the body of Jean Hartley, a cheerleader from Palisades High, had been found in the woods near Secca Lake.

Jessica shuddered. Finding Dean Maddingly's body had been dreadful, but this was a hundred times worse because everyone knew the girl lying on the floor. Katrina had been visiting from San Francisco for the past few weeks and had attended classes with Amy at SVH. She was an outgoing, likable person who had made friends easily.

Jonathan walked over to Katrina and Elizabeth and crouched down beside them. He moved with a strength and grace that took Jessica's breath away, even in the midst of the horror. She felt a glimmer of hope as she watched him pick up Katrina's limp arm and press his fingers against the girl's throat. *Jonathan can do just about anything,* Jessica thought proudly. She was sure that if anyone could save Katrina's life, he could.

But Jonathan released his hold on the girl's arm, letting it flop back down to the floor. "It's no use, Elizabeth," he said, shaking his head. "She's dead."

*   *   *

Enid Rollins hovered in the corner of the drafty living room, her whole body trembling. The sight of Jonathan and Jessica descending the stairs together like a king and queen had shattered Enid's heart. *How could you do this to me, Jonathan?* she silently cried. *Don't you know how much I love you?*

Enid absently noted the commotion in the room. Amy Sutton was crying hysterically, her cousin was lying on the floor, and Elizabeth was administering CPR, even though it was obvious that the girl didn't stand a chance.

Some party! Enid raged to herself. *Katrina Sutton dropped dead, and Jessica stole Jonathan away from me.* The night was a total bust. Just as Enid wondered what could happen to make things worse, the shrill wail of sirens sliced through the chaos. Blinking lights flashed through the windows.

"The ambulance is here!" someone shouted. "And the police!"

Enid's mind was in a haze as she watched the scene unfold like a movie. The front door of the mansion burst open, and the gruff voices of police officers filled the room, shouting orders. A team of emergency medical technicians rushed in behind them and surrounded Katrina's still body.

The room grew silent. Enid watched Jonathan's expression, noting how strong he appeared. *He's*

9

always in control, she thought. Despite the terrible way he had treated her, she couldn't help still being attracted to him.

From the moment she first laid eyes on Jonathan Cain, Enid had been sure he was her soul mate. She'd tried everything to make him realize how perfect they were for each other. She had changed herself completely, dyeing her light reddish brown hair jet black and adopting the gothic look that Jonathan seemed to prefer.

Enid was totally devoted to him and didn't care what others thought about her obsession. Nothing was more important than her soul mate—not friends, not family, not schoolwork. She'd chased him shamelessly, without a thought to her own pride. When her former best friend, Elizabeth Wakefield, had spread vicious lies about Jonathan, Enid had dropped her like a rancid potato.

Even now, after he'd broken her heart with Jessica, Enid wasn't ready to give up on Jonathan. *I love him too much,* she realized.

Within seconds the EMS guys established that Katrina Sutton was indeed dead. Two of the police officers hovered over the girl's body, speaking softly, but their voices were loud enough for Enid to overhear the words "just like the others."

One of the police officers rose to his feet and addressed the group. "I'm Detective Roger Marsh of the Sweet Valley Police Department, and this is Officer Reyes," he added, gesturing toward the uniformed policeman with him. "It looks as though this girl was killed by the same person who has committed two other similar murders in the past few weeks."

A collective gasp sounded from the group. Across the room, Jessica buried her face in Jonathan's shoulder. Enid sank to the floor by the wall, a wrenching pain slicing through her gut. The murder hardly seemed real at all, but seeing Jonathan and Jessica together shattered Enid's soul.

I'm going home, she decided. The loss of Jonathan was an open wound, and she longed to nurse her aching heart in solitude. Bracing herself against the wall, Enid rose to her feet. But when she moved toward the door, another police officer stopped her.

"I'm sorry, miss. I can't let you leave just yet." Then he turned to the group. "No one is to leave the premises until they've been questioned. Please be patient. With everyone's cooperation, we'll get you out of here as quickly as possible."

Enid whirled around and returned to the living room, where she plopped herself down on a tattered sofa next to the fireplace. A cloud of dust rose from the cushions. *Would Jonathan love me again if I helped him clean up this place?* she wondered hopefully. *I'm sure Jessica would never think of that trick.*

The police began herding the kids into various rooms off the living room for questioning. Enid leaned back and closed her eyes, imagining the grateful look on Jonathan's face when she offered to vacuum and dust after the party.

Chapter 2

Todd drove Elizabeth home from the party, steering his BMW with one hand while the other was loosely entwined with hers. Neither of them spoke, but it was different from the stony, oppressive silences of their last few dates.

As the car passed under a streetlight, Todd studied her profile. Elizabeth seemed so scared and upset, her blue-green eyes shining with tears. Seeing her like that tugged at his heart.

Although Elizabeth had caused their recent breakup by cheating on him with a guy she'd met at summer camp in Montana, Todd couldn't help his feelings for her. Even after he'd caught her kissing the creep, Todd still cared, and he probably always would.

Remembering that horrible night, Todd tightened

his grip on the steering wheel. He'd arrived at Elizabeth's house to find her in Joey Mason's arms. For days afterward, Todd had walked around like a volcano ready to erupt. He'd decided to make some changes in his life, starting with his sappy, nice-guy image.

Todd had put on a tougher, macho-man look, dyeing his hair black, wearing a black leather jacket, and going around with his face unshaven. It had worked—up to a point. Girls had begun paying more attention to him at school, boosting his ego sky-high. For a while he'd managed to convince himself that he was better off without Elizabeth.

But now, after the horror they'd been through at Jonathan's house that evening, Todd felt closer to Elizabeth than he had in a long time. He admitted to himself that he'd never stopped loving her.

At a red light, Todd brought Elizabeth's hand to his lips and planted a gentle kiss on her wrist. He heard her sigh, and his heart melted, along with the last of his anger. Todd wanted to put the whole mess behind them and move forward with Elizabeth. He resolved to give her another chance, to forgive her for Joey Mason. He didn't care if getting back together with her might make him look like a sap—Elizabeth was much more important to him than any image. It was obvious to him that they belonged together.

As he turned onto Calico Drive, Todd took a deep breath. "Elizabeth," he whispered, glancing at her again.

She turned to him, and their eyes met briefly. Todd smiled, suddenly feeling very happy and relieved at the thought of having Elizabeth back in his life. *I've really missed her,* he realized. But just as he was about to tell her so, he noticed Joey Mason's Land Rover parked in the Wakefields' driveway.

Todd let go of her hand and slammed on the brakes, the tires screeching to a dead stop.

Elizabeth's eyes narrowed in a questioning look. "What's the matter?" she asked softly.

As if you didn't know, he retorted inwardly, squeezing the steering wheel as he would have liked to squeeze Joey Mason's throat at that moment.

"Todd?" Elizabeth whispered.

"You're home," he snapped.

She gave him a long, probing look, then stepped out of the car. Immediately Todd took off down the road, anxious to put distance between them. *Once a sap, always a sap,* he berated himself.

A few blocks away, Todd pulled over and rolled down the window. "When will I ever learn?" he shouted, slamming his hand on the steering wheel. His whole body was shaking. He sucked in deep gulps of the moist night air, trying to make himself calm down enough to drive safely. *I can't believe I even considered forgiving her,* he thought.

Jonathan sat in the kitchen with two police officers, staring at them across the table. Everyone else had left, and now it was his turn to be interrogated by Sweet Valley's finest.

Detective Marsh ran his hand over his thinning hair as Officer Reyes flipped through his notes. "OK, Jonathan, let's go over this one more time," Reyes said, looking directly at him. "You left the living room just before the lights went out?"

Jonathan kept his expression even and calm. "*As* the lights went out, is what I believe I said. I can't remember exactly where my feet were at the precise moment of the blackout." He was sure that Jessica's statement would back up his own.

Officer Reyes flipped to another page of his notebook. "You say your parents are in Europe at this time, on business?"

"For a few weeks," Jonathan replied, trying not to sound bored. He was getting tired of repeating the same information. "Would you like a cup of coffee, some wine perhaps?" he offered, pleased with the gracious tone of his voice. Although the kitchen was still quite bare, Jonathan had managed to find a stove and refrigerator that worked. It was enough to make the room appear functional.

Officer Reyes's eyes narrowed. "We take underage drinking very seriously around here," he warned.

Jonathan raised his hands and shook his head. "And I would never touch the stuff, but I found a bottle of old wine in an upstairs closet. The previous owners of this house probably left it behind."

"Where are your parents right now?" Detective Marsh interjected.

"In Germany," Jonathan replied evenly.

"Where in Germany?" the detective asked.

Jonathan ran his finger over his bottom lip. "I don't know exactly. They left the village of Mainz today and should be arriving in Kiel in a few hours. I'm sure they'll call me from there."

Officer Reyes's eyebrows rose sharply. "You're saying you don't have a phone number to reach them?"

Jonathan shook his head. "I'm afraid not."

"What exactly is the nature of your parents' work in Europe?" Detective Marsh asked.

Jonathan clenched his fists under the table,

struggling to keep his temper under control. "I mentioned it earlier. My parents are musicologists, currently conducting research on a cache of music manuscripts that was recently discovered in an abandoned farmhouse in Germany."

"We'd like to speak with your parents as soon as possible." Reyes snapped his notebook shut and turned to his colleague. Both officers seemed satisfied.

"I'll tell them to call the police station as soon as I hear from them," Jonathan assured them.

"You do that," Detective Marsh replied. "And remember, there's a ten o'clock curfew in effect until all this trouble is over. No more late-night parties."

Jonathan bowed his head and looked up at the officers with an expression of sincerity. "Don't worry, sir. It'll never happen again. I promise."

"See that it doesn't," Reyes added.

After he'd walked the police officers to the front door, Jonathan shuffled through the huge, empty house, shutting off the lights. As he returned to the living room, he pulled down a green streamer dangling from the ceiling.

A few colorful balloons still decorated the walls, although most of the party debris had been cleared away by Enid Rollins, one of his hopeless admirers. He chuckled as he recalled how difficult it had been to get rid of Enid that evening. The foolish girl had *demanded* the privilege of serving as his housemaid.

Jonathan picked up the iron poker and crouched down before the fireplace. Slowly he began to stir the dying embers. It had been an interesting night, but he knew the time was quickly approaching when he'd have to leave Sweet Valley. Normally the thought wouldn't have bothered him at all. He made it a rule never to become attached to people, no matter how much they fawned over him.

There was only one person keeping him in Sweet Valley. Thinking of Jessica, Jonathan hung his head and moaned aloud, the sound reverberating through the drafty room. *How can I tear myself away from her?* he agonized.

Jessica Wakefield had managed to wedge herself into his life—and his heart—in a way no girl had in a long, long time. He tried to push away the image of her as she'd been that evening—beautiful, as always, and so sweet and willing. Jonathan glanced up at the portrait above the fireplace. Even in the shadows, the painted eyes seemed to be gazing down at him with scorn.

I should have left this place days ago, he told himself. He crushed out the last of the fire, wishing he could do the same to the one that burned in his heart. All of a sudden a small, cunning voice in his head asked, *But why leave her behind? Why not take Jessica away with me?*

"Sharing my life with Jessica," he whispered, tempted by the idea of having her at his side forever. Her beauty and vivaciousness could make his world bright again. Maybe he could find the joy he'd lost.

Immediately he rose and threw the poker across the room. It banged into the plaster wall and landed with a loud thump on the hardwood floor. *Jessica belongs right where she is, in her own world,* Jonathan warned himself. *And don't you forget it!*

Suddenly there was a soft, creaking step on the front porch. Jonathan jerked his head around, his body tense and his senses alert. His heart throbbed painfully as he waited.

Someone knocked at the door. "Jonathan?" she called.

"Jessica," he groaned, instantly recognizing the sweet, feminine voice. He held his breath and forced himself to remain still.

She banged on the door again, louder.

He clenched his fists at his sides, striving for control. *Leave, Jessica,* he thought, *before it's too late!*

She banged again, thumping hard enough to rattle the walls. Jonathan smiled tenderly as he pictured Jessica standing on the other side of the door, trying to kick her way through to him. "What am I going to do with her?" he whispered, shaking his head.

"Please let me in, Jonathan," she pleaded.

Jonathan exhaled sharply, his hands trembling. His honorable intentions crumbled to dust. Cursing himself and his weakness, he rushed to answer the door.

"It must've been horrible," Joey said, pulling Elizabeth into his arms. They were sitting side by side on the front steps of the Wakefields' split-level home, talking about what had happened at Jonathan's house that evening.

"It was. Katrina's body was so horribly white—" Elizabeth shuddered. "And the police still don't know who's committing these horrible murders."

Joey brushed his hand across the back of her neck and kissed the side of her head. "It's OK," he whispered comfortingly.

Elizabeth looked into his emerald green eyes and sighed. She could just make out the outline of his sharp features in the dark. *He really is gorgeous,* she thought.

"I was pretty angry at you for not asking me to go with you to the party," he admitted. "But considering how badly it turned out . . ." His voice trailed off as he lowered his lips to hers.

Elizabeth closed her eyes and tried to lose herself in Joey's kiss, but worry and confusion stalked through her thoughts. She suspected his presence was the reason Todd had stormed off in such a hurry.

Joey pulled back and hooked his finger under her chin. "You're really upset, aren't you?" he asked gently.

She nodded, her eyes filling with tears. "And I still have a feeling Jessica is in big trouble at this very minute, even though I'm sure she went home with Amy after the party." Elizabeth sighed and shook her head. "Maybe my twin radar is stuck."

Joey dropped a brief kiss on her lips. "Did anyone ever tell you that you worry too much?"

Elizabeth smiled sheepishly. "Only everyone."

He chuckled softly and rose to his feet, pulling her up beside him. "I recommend a good night's sleep and hot, heavy dreams about me." He winked. "I'll call you tomorrow and you can tell me all about them."

After Joey left, Elizabeth went inside and plunked herself down on the living room couch, determined to wait up for her sister. Their parents had gone out for the evening and wouldn't be back for hours.

Elizabeth's gut kept flashing a warning that her twin was in danger. *But Jessica isn't in trouble,* she mentally argued. Amy had been shaken up terribly by her cousin's murder, and Jessica had offered to stay with her for a while.

Maybe I do worry too much, Elizabeth thought, doubting herself. *But it sure feels like Jessica needs me right now.*

Chapter 3

Jessica crossed her arms and glared impatiently at Jonathan. She'd been sitting on the dilapidated couch in his living room since she arrived, waiting for him to stop poking at the fire he was building in the fireplace. "Maybe I should have stayed at Amy's house," she complained.

Jonathan glanced at her over his shoulder, his expression masked. "I agree."

Jessica's eyes filled with tears. "A few hours ago I thought you really cared. I guess I was wrong." She took a deep, shaky breath and rose to her feet. "I'm leaving."

"No!" Jonathan shouted. In the span of a heartbeat, he was by her side, pulling her into his arms. "Jessica, I love you so much, it hurts."

She held him close, pressing her hands against

his lean back. "Then why do you keep pushing me away?" she cried.

Jonathan moaned as if he were in pain. "I push you away because I love you."

"That doesn't make sense!" she snapped.

Jonathan touched her lips with his finger, stilling her protests. "Maybe you're right," he replied. He traced a line over her chin, down her neck. A strange fire burned in his eyes, hotter than the one in the hearth. He combed his fingers through her hair and pushed it back from her face. "I do love you, Jessica," he said, lowering his lips to hers.

As the kiss went on and on, Jessica felt herself being pulled into a hot whirlpool of sensations. She couldn't think straight, and her heart felt as if it were about to explode.

Jonathan raised his head and looked into her eyes, capturing her with the intensity of his gaze. "I'm going to show you something wonderful," he promised.

Jessica swallowed hard, suddenly terrified of his power over her. She finally understood with gut certainty that, whether she wanted to or not, she would never be able to escape Jonathan.

"It's OK, my love," he murmured soothingly, as if he'd read her thoughts.

Jessica trembled as he kissed her again. Closing her eyes, she drifted into a pool of sweet bliss. Her fears melted away like warm honey.

His lips blazed a hot trail of kisses down her neck, nipping at her heated skin. "You belong to me, Jessica," he murmured, his voice thick with passion. "For these few moments, you will be mine."

Jessica tilted her head in response, welcoming him. "Oh, yes," she murmured, her heart throbbing. "I want to belong to you forever, Jonathan." Her mind began spinning, and a sense of weightlessness came over her. She felt as if she were floating, fluttering on a breeze like a feather. A gust of cool wind whipped through her hair, taking her breath away. She was afraid, but incredibly excited.

"Open your eyes," she heard Jonathan say.

Jessica immediately obeyed. At first she saw nothing, as though she were soaring through a sea of blackness. The air smelled sweet and fresh, heavy with the salty scent of the ocean. As Jessica's eyes began to focus, she gasped. A million tiny lights sparkled below her. "Jonathan, what's happening?" she shrieked. She turned to him, and for a moment she found herself looking into the jet black eyes of a raven.

Jessica opened her mouth to scream, but then the bird's eyes turned blue and she was looking into Jonathan's face.

"Don't be afraid," he whispered.

Lulled by his reassuring words, Jessica nodded. She looked around and saw that she was still sitting on his lap in the living room of the old mansion. But when she buried her face in the crook of his shoulder, she felt as though she were resting her head in a pile of soft, downy feathers. The sensation of soaring through the night sky returned. *Maybe I'm losing my mind,* she told herself. *But I don't care.*

"I love you, Jessica," Jonathan whispered, his soft breath tickling her ear. Then he was kissing her again, and Jessica felt as if she were falling out of the sky like a shooting star. In the next moment, she was aware of the damp ground under her back, her arms wrapped tightly around Jonathan and her heart ready to burst with happiness. The fragrance of wildflowers hung in the air, enveloping her in a cloud of sweet perfume.

Jonathan brushed his lips across her face, dropping featherlight kisses on her eyelids, her chin, her neck. He gently teased the sensitive spot below her jaw, where her pulse was jumping wildly.

Jessica's eyes filled with tears as her heart overflowed with tenderness and love. She wrapped her arms around Jonathan and turned her head, silently urging him to continue.

Jonathan groaned and pressed harder, sucking hungrily at her neck. "Oh, yes," Jessica gasped, digging her fingers into the soft dirt at her sides. She felt as though hot syrup were pulsing through her veins.

A sense of tingling delight began to flow through her. The pleasure grew slowly at first, then faster, until the whole world was spinning out of control. She could feel Jonathan's heart pounding as fast as her own. An incredible need blazed through her, engulfing her body, her mind, her very soul.

"Jonathan," Jessica moaned softly, running her fingers through his dark silky hair. She hungrily kissed his neck, his ear, his lips. "I love you, Jonathan." Then everything went black.

Elizabeth paced back and forth across the living room, pausing every now and then to gaze out the window. It was long past midnight, and she was growing more and more frantic as she waited for Jessica to come home.

"I should have gone with her," Elizabeth mumbled, clenching her fists. She followed her path back to the window and absently pulled aside the edge of the curtain. *Where are you, Jess?* she wondered desperately.

She glanced outside and gasped. The twins' black Jeep Wrangler was parked in the driveway. Elizabeth reeled back, as if she'd been splashed in the face with a bucket of ice water. The Jeep hadn't been there the last time she'd checked. *This can't be,* she thought.

She ran upstairs to her sister's room and threw open the door. A Jessica-sized lump in the bed stirred. *It just can't be her,* Elizabeth's mind argued. She switched on the light. The "lump" had long blond hair and Jessica's face.

A feeling of cold dread crept along Elizabeth's spine as she stared at her sleeping twin. *How did Jessica get by me?* she wondered. There was no logical explanation.

"I *don't* worry too much," Elizabeth whispered, thinking of what Joey had said earlier. She was absolutely convinced that Jessica had been in terrible danger that night. *And she still is,* Elizabeth thought.

Jessica felt as if she'd slept for a hundred years when she woke up the following day. Slowly she sat up in her bed and stretched. Her mind was in a fog, but a delicious warmth radiated through her whole body. She settled back against her pillow and sighed. "Jonathan," she whispered, smiling.

She recalled the passion in his kisses, the strength of his arms around her. But some of the details of the previous evening seemed hazy, as if parts of her brain were shrouded in thick clouds. She couldn't even remember driving home. "I *did* go back to Jonathan's after I left Amy's house—didn't I?"

As she struggled to piece together the puzzle of

her memory, a few crazy images popped into her mind. *Flying with a bird and landing in a field of wildflowers?* she thought, giggling. *Talk about wild dreams!*

From downstairs came the enticing aroma of breakfast—coffee, bacon, and pancakes. Jessica took a deep breath and grinned, positive that it was going to be a wonderful day.

A few minutes later she plodded downstairs to the kitchen, where her twin and parents were already gathered at the butcher block table. "Good morning, everyone," Jessica chirped.

Three pairs of somber eyes stared back at her. Jessica blinked, nonplussed. For a moment she couldn't understand what had put everyone in such a bad mood. Then she glanced at the front page of the *Sweet Valley News,* which was on the table, and scanned the headline: "Serial Killer Claims Third Victim—Teenage Visitor from San Francisco."

How could I have forgotten that Amy's cousin was murdered last night? Jessica wondered, shaking her head. It seemed that the thrill of getting together with Jonathan had overshadowed everything else in her mind.

"What a tragedy," she murmured as she sat down at the table. "Poor Amy. She was really upset last night." Jessica helped herself to two pancakes and some bacon, then impulsively added another pancake to her plate. "I'm starving this morning," she declared.

"It certainly is a tragedy," her mother agreed emphatically. "I'm terribly disappointed in you girls for putting yourselves in danger."

Jessica washed down a mouthful of food with a gulp of orange juice and looked up. "What do you mean?"

"What I mean is this." Alice Wakefield firmly set down her coffee cup before continuing, obviously very upset. "My daughters went to a party last night, after curfew, and a girl was murdered there." Her voice began to tremble. "You should have known better. There's a serial killer on the loose. When I think what might have happened if—" Her voice broke on a sob.

Ned Wakefield rubbed his wife's shoulder, then picked up where she'd left off. "The town curfew is for your own protection," he lectured. "That doesn't seem to be such a hard concept to understand, but apparently the kids of Sweet Valley just don't get it. Especially the guy who threw the party—what's his name?"

"Jonathan Cain," Elizabeth murmured.

Jonathan Cain, Jessica echoed in her mind. A warm tingle shimmied up and down her spine.

"Jonathan Cain," her father spat, as if it were a foul word. "He exposed everyone to serious danger by deciding to ignore the curfew and have a party. Obviously he's either a troublemaker or just not very bright." Mr. Wakefield glared at Elizabeth and Jessica. "But that doesn't excuse the two of you," he continued. "You girls should have known better than to break curfew and go to that party. I'm holding you both entirely responsible for your actions."

Jessica forced herself to maintain a somber expression, despite the fact that inside she was dancing for joy. *Jonathan is mine at last,* her mind sang.

"Katrina's funeral will be held on Monday," Mrs. Wakefield mentioned, her eyes scanning the front-page article. "It says here that school will be canceled for the day."

Jessica was about to cheer for that bit of good news, but she caught the impulse in time. Biting down hard on her bottom lip, she helped herself to more bacon. "Thanks to whoever made this fabulous breakfast," she said enthusiastically. "It's delicious!"

Elizabeth glanced at her with a wry expression. "You're welcome," she muttered.

"Katrina is going to be buried in the Sutton family plot," their mother continued. "I don't even want to imagine the anguish and heartache that poor girl's parents are suffering right now." Her eyes filled with tears. "And to think it could have been either of you." She reached out and squeezed Jessica's and Elizabeth's hands.

"But it wasn't," Jessica replied.

Ned Wakefield scowled at her, his blue eyes shining with anger. Jessica ducked her head sheepishly. *I guess that wasn't the right thing to say,* she thought.

"You're not going to take any more foolish chances," he announced. "You girls are grounded at night for two weeks."

Jessica gasped in disbelief. *Grounded?* she thought. *They can't!* She glanced at her twin, hoping for an ally, but Elizabeth looked terribly guilty—and sorrowful. *I'm on my own,* Jessica told herself as she turned back to her father. "Every single night for two entire weeks?" she protested.

Her father's nostrils flared. "That's right. From sunset to morning, for two weeks. And Jonathan Cain's house is *entirely* off-limits."

Jessica's jaw dropped. "For the whole two weeks?" she cried.

Her father's eyes narrowed. "Depending on your attitude, it could be extended to three weeks, or four. . . ."

Jessica raised her hands in surrender. "Two weeks are enough. But we can still have people over, right?"

"As long as they leave in time to make the curfew," her mother replied.

"But we could have a pool party or something?"

34

Jessica asked eagerly. She imagined Jonathan's reaction to her new blue bikini and shivered with delicious anticipation.

Elizabeth gaped at her. "Amy's cousin died last night. I don't think anyone is in the mood for a pool party."

Jessica blinked, momentarily surprised. "That's right. What was I thinking? A party wouldn't be very cool at all. Anyway, the only person I'm anxious to see is Jonathan." She stabbed a forkful of pancakes and swirled it through a puddle of maple syrup.

"No," Ned Wakefield responded tersely. "I don't want either of you to go anywhere near him."

Jessica jerked her head up, horrified. "What? You only said that we can't go to his house."

"I don't think he's the kind of guy you should be spending your time with," her father argued. "Jonathan Cain obviously doesn't have any regard for others, and I forbid you to see him. Period."

Jessica glared at him, her eyes burning with tears.

Her father's expression remained hard. "If you girls aren't willing to demonstrate some common sense on your own, your mother and I are going to step in and do it for you."

Alice Wakefield rose to her feet. "Anyone want more coffee?" she offered.

Elizabeth held up her cup. "I do."

Jessica sat in silent anguish, her whole body

throbbing with wrenching pain as everyone went back to eating pancakes and sipping coffee. *As if they didn't just destroy my whole life,* she thought, trembling.

She twisted her napkin into a tight rope on her lap, winding it around her wrist. Her palms were sweating. A feeling of panic crashed over her, roaring in her ears. Her breathing became labored, as if she were suffocating. *Do they really expect me to survive without Jonathan?* she wondered.

Finally something inside Jessica exploded. "No!" she screamed, banging her elbows on the table. "You can't do this to me!"

Chapter 4

Elizabeth gulped in a quick breath of utter astonishment as she watched her twin's hysterical out-
burst.

"I can't believe you're punishing me for what
happened to Katrina!" Jessica raged. "It's not fair,
it's not fair, it's not *fair!*" She tugged at her hair,
sobbing and gasping as she whipped her head
from side to side. "You don't even know him!" she
wailed.

What's wrong *with her?* Elizabeth wondered,
totally horrified. Jessica had always had a flair for
the dramatic, but Elizabeth couldn't remember
ever seeing her so out of control. *She's carrying on
as if her* life *depended on being with Jonathan,*
Elizabeth realized.

Although most of the kids at Sweet Valley

High had been fawning over him and copying his creepy, gothic style, Elizabeth couldn't understand the attraction. She'd disliked Jonathan Cain the instant she first saw him, and in the weeks since, he hadn't done a single thing to make her stop loathing him. Now, seeing her twin's red, blotchy face and hearing her mournful cries, Elizabeth felt disgusted. Jessica's passion seemed so . . . *unnatural,* as if Jonathan had cast an evil spell over her.

"If you would just meet him!" Jessica pleaded. "He's the most intelligent, refined guy I've ever known. He gets straight A's, and even the teachers are amazed at how smart he is. He's traveled all over the world; he's so cultured, but he's not a snob."

Elizabeth saw a pained look flicker across her mother's face. "Jessica, he may be a fine person," Alice Wakefield conceded in a soft, gentle voice. "But the party—"

Jessica slammed her hand on the table. "The party wasn't even his idea!" she hollered. "The other guys—Bruce, Winston, *Todd*—they're the ones who insisted that Jonathan have that stupid party!"

Elizabeth felt a warm, tender sensation at the mention of Todd's name. Something special had passed between them the night before. He'd been so gentle and understanding. *Do I still love him?* she wondered.

"Jonathan was pressured into having the party," Jessica explained, somewhat calmer. "He didn't want to disappoint everyone. That's no reason to keep me from seeing him. At least let him come over for dinner or something. That way you can check him out for yourselves."

Their father set his coffee cup down and folded his hands. "I appreciate what you're saying, Jessica, but I don't want to discuss this further."

Alice Wakefield covered his hand with her own. "Ned, maybe we should reconsider."

"What do you mean?" he asked. "Don't tell me you're willing to let our daughters go back to that place, given what's happened. What's wrong with his parents, anyway, letting him stay in California while they're traveling around Europe?"

I wouldn't go back to that creepy mansion for a million dollars, Elizabeth thought.

"I agree that his house should be off-limits," her mother said. "But I don't see anything wrong with allowing the boy to come over for dinner."

"There's *nothing* wrong with it!" Jessica exclaimed. "It would be so great if we could have him over for Sunday dinner. I'm sure it's been a long time since he's had a decent home-cooked meal."

Elizabeth saw her father's expression soften, and her stomach tightened. *Please don't say yes,*

Dad, she hoped. *Jonathan Cain is a walking horror!*
If there was anything she could add to the discussion to persuade her parents to keep Jonathan away from Jessica, she'd say it. But blurting out her opinion of him, without any facts to back it up, wouldn't be much of an argument. And besides, Jessica would rip her head off.

"Come on, Ned," her mother said. "Let's have Jonathan over for dinner tomorrow night. We'll meet him and see for ourselves whether or not he's the kind of guy Jessica should date."

Ned Wakefield exhaled noisily. "It looks like I'm outnumbered here."

Jessica's tears dried up immediately. "That's all I ask," she replied, flashing her parents a watery smile.

Elizabeth bit her lip to keep it from trembling. Just imagining Jonathan's feverish blue eyes and pale white skin gave her a queasy feeling. She certainly wasn't thrilled about having him in her home.

"I think we should have chicken with mushrooms in that creamy wine sauce that Elizabeth knows how to make," Jessica remarked cheerfully, turning to Elizabeth with a huge smile. "What do you say?"

Elizabeth shrugged and pushed a piece of bacon around her plate. "I suppose."

Jessica clapped her hands and rubbed them together vigorously. "Great! And I'm going to make a totally awesome dessert, except I'm not sure what. Frozen chocolate-walnut pie would be nice. Or maybe we should have something more sophisticated, like crepes. How about chocolate crepes with white chocolate mousse and fruit salsa?"

Her mother laughed. "Looks like a trip to Season's Gourmet Shop is in order."

Jessica sighed. "I want everything to be perfect."

"It'll be loaded down with fat and sugar, at least," Elizabeth added wryly.

"Fat and sugar is OK for such a special occasion," her twin replied, giving Elizabeth a narrow-eyed look before turning back to her parents. "I can't wait for you two to meet him," Jessica gushed. "Jonathan's parents are so wrapped up in their work, they don't seem to pay much attention to him. He's made me realize how lucky I am to have parents who love me enough to be here for me when I need them."

Elizabeth groaned to herself. She knew exactly what her twin was up to with all the flattery. In the next instant her suspicion was confirmed.

"I only wish I could buy a new dress for the occasion," Jessica lamented. "You know, to make the whole thing more . . . festive."

41

"You have lots of pretty outfits," her mother pointed out. "If you'd clean your room and straighten your closet, I'm sure you'd find clothes you've forgotten you owned. It would be like acquiring a whole new wardrobe."

"Oh, I know I have lots of nice things," Jessica drawled. "But buying a new outfit would make the evening even more special. Like a real dinner party."

Elizabeth rolled her eyes, watching as Jessica managed to weasel the use of a credit card out of her dad.

"But you're still grounded," he reminded the twins sternly.

"Yes, Dad," Jessica chimed.

After breakfast Jessica bolted from the kitchen, claiming she had a million things to do in preparation for Sunday dinner. Determined to get some straight answers, Elizabeth followed. She marched into her twin's room and shut the door.

Jessica turned to her and smiled. "I'm glad you're here, Liz. You can help me put together the grocery list for tomorrow."

Elizabeth crossed her arms. "What's going on, Jess?"

"Sunday dinner." Jessica laughed, shaking her head. "And I thought *I* had memory problems."

"What time did you get home last night?"

Elizabeth demanded. "And where were you?"

Jessica plopped down on her bed. "I didn't look at the clock when I got in, I was at Amy's house, and as far as I can tell, you're playing police interrogator." She flashed a snide grin. "It's been lots of fun, Liz, but now you can leave. I don't have time for games."

Elizabeth glared at her. "Don't you? What about your explosion in the kitchen a few minutes ago? What kind of a hold does Jonathan Cain have on you, Jess?"

Jessica's defiant expression softened. For an instant Elizabeth thought she saw a glimmer of terror in her sister's eyes. "I'm in love with Jonathan," Jessica replied defensively. "I guess because you're so mixed up about Todd and Joey, you just can't understand how it is to love only one guy."

Elizabeth flinched as if she'd been slapped. "That's not fair, and you know it!"

Jessica leaned over the edge of the mattress and began rummaging through a pile of clothes on the floor next to the bed. "Maybe you should stick to your own guy problems and let me worry about mine."

"There's just no getting through to you!" Elizabeth exclaimed in frustration.

Jessica pulled out a lime green tunic and held it

43

up for inspection. "I'm not sure if I still like this color," she remarked. "What do you think?"

Elizabeth threw up her arms and pulled open the door. "I think you're headed for disaster," she said over her shoulder.

Elizabeth went back downstairs to help her parents clean up the kitchen. *Maybe I should let them know how I feel about Jonathan,* she thought. But she immediately dropped the idea. In fairness to both twins, their parents wouldn't take her word over Jessica's. And besides, it wouldn't be right for Elizabeth to go behind her sister's back. Wrong or right, the Wakefield twins stuck together.

The phone rang, cutting into Elizabeth's thoughts. She answered it and was slightly disappointed to hear Joey's voice on the line. *Who was I expecting—Todd?* she asked herself pointedly.

"How were your dreams last night?" Joey asked in a low, intimate voice.

Elizabeth blinked, bemused. "My dreams?"

He chuckled softly. "You were supposed to have hot dreams about me, remember?"

Elizabeth squeezed her bottom lip between her teeth. After the harrowing morning she'd had, and the prospect of Jonathan coming to her house for dinner, she wasn't in the mood for teasing banter with Joey. But she realized it wasn't fair to take her problems out on him. She took a deep breath, forcing herself to relax.

"Actually, my dreams must have been very boring," she said. "I slept right through them."

Joey laughed at her joke. Then his voice became serious. "I heard about your party on the news this morning."

"I'm still rather shaken up about the whole thing," Elizabeth murmured.

"I've got the perfect solution to help take your mind off it," Joey remarked cheerfully. "There's a new play opening at the regional theater tonight. I have no idea what it's about, but my comparative literature professor wrote it. It might help my grade to go see it, with extra credit for bringing you along."

Elizabeth switched the call to the portable phone and stepped outside to the patio, where she could speak privately. "I'd really like to, but I can't tonight."

A wary tone crept into his voice. "Are you having second thoughts about us?" he asked. "Should I be jealous because Todd Wilkins drove you home last night? I wasn't going to mention it, but . . ."

"No, of course not." Elizabeth sat down on a lawn chair and closed her eyes. "It's just that . . . I'm grounded." Her face grew hot with embarrassment.

"Grounded!" Joey shrieked. "That's so . . . *high school!*"

Elizabeth leaned forward and rested her elbows on her knees. "Yes, well, I *am* in high school, Joey. Remember?"

"Can't you get out of it?"

Elizabeth sniffed. "I don't think so."

"Why don't you make up something?" he suggested.

"Like what?" she asked flatly.

"I don't know . . . tell them it's my parents' anniversary and they're flying out from New York to meet you."

Elizabeth shifted nervously in the chair. "I couldn't do that, Joey."

He laughed. "Yeah, I guess not. You're a terrible liar, aren't you?"

She winced, picking up his reference to the lie she'd told him about Jonathan's party. Joey had asked her to go out with him on the same night, but she'd made up a story about having promised to go to a movie with Jessica. Within minutes of telling him, though, Elizabeth had been exposed by the biggest gossip in Sweet Valley High, Caroline Pearce. "I guess I'm doomed to an honest life," Elizabeth quipped, trying to make light of the embarrassing incident.

"I know," Joey said. "It's only one of the things I love about you. But I miss you, Elizabeth."

She looked across the yard, hesitating for an

instant. "Would you like to come over for dinner tomorrow?"

"Just you and me?" he asked in a hopeful tone.

"And my family," she clarified. "And Jessica's new boyfr—*person*." Elizabeth grimaced. Her mind refused to think of Jonathan as her twin's boyfriend.

Joey sighed dramatically. "Sunday dinner with the folks wasn't exactly what I had in mind," he complained. "But I'll take what I can get. You're worth it, Elizabeth."

She smiled at the compliment. "Thanks, Joey."

After they hung up, Elizabeth leaned back and gazed at the few wispy clouds in the sky. When she'd first met Joey at Camp Echo Mountain in Montana, he had seemed larger than life. She'd fallen instantly in love with him, melting at the very sight of his emerald green eyes and wide, sexy smile.

Joey had directed the play Elizabeth had written during her stay at camp. She planned to become a professional writer someday, and his encouragement and praise of her work had meant a lot to her. Elizabeth was on the staff of Sweet Valley High's student newspaper, the *Oracle*, for which she wrote a regular column called "Personal Profiles." But working on *Summer Love* with Joey had been an entirely different creative experience.

Not to mention all the nights we sneaked out of our cabins to be together, she thought.

Elizabeth had tried to forget him when she'd returned from Camp Echo Mountain. But Joey had transferred to UCLA recently, putting him within driving distance of Sweet Valley. Elizabeth had found herself irresistibly attracted to him, and her relationship with Todd had quickly fallen apart.

So why didn't I ask Joey to go with me to Jonathan's party? she wondered. *And why can't I stop thinking about Todd?*

Jessica smiled triumphantly as she walked out of the Valley Mall later that afternoon, carrying several packages. She'd bought a gorgeous lilac silk dress that fit as if it had been made especially for her. The soft fabric would show off her willowy curves and shimmer when she moved. Then, with a bit of perseverance, Jessica had found just the right accessories: a silver chain belt, dressy leather sandals—on sale for thirty percent off—and a pale mauve lipstick that complemented the dress perfectly.

And because she'd saved so much on the shoes, Jessica had treated herself to a second outfit: a gray and black striped dress and a black satin vest to wear to Katrina Sutton's funeral on Monday.

Jessica tossed her packages into the backseat of the Jeep. Turning out of the parking lot, she impulsively headed toward Jonathan's house. Even though her parents had declared it off-limits, Jessica couldn't stop herself. She felt drawn to the place—and to Jonathan. Something wonderful had happened between them the night before, and her heart fluttered in anticipation as she turned onto Forrest Lane.

But when she arrived at Jonathan's house and hopped out of the Jeep, she hesitated. Shading her eyes with her hand, she stared at the crumbling old mansion. Several windows were boarded up, and the gray paint was cracked and peeling. Most of the shutters dangled loosely from their hinges, swinging against the house with the slightest breeze. The front porch sagged at a noticeable angle. The steps had several gaping holes, like the sinister smile of a jack-o'-lantern.

Jessica shivered. *It really is a creepy house,* she reflected. *And less than twenty-four hours ago, a murder took place here!* She recalled the image of Katrina's body lying on the floor, her wavy blond hair fanned out like a halo around her pale face.

Poor Jonathan, Jessica thought. *It must be just horrible for him to stay in this house after what happened.* For his sake, she resolved to be strong.

Steeling her nerves, she marched up to the front door and rapped firmly with the ornate brass knocker.

As she waited for Jonathan to answer, Jessica became increasingly aware of how desolate the area was. Small noises seemed sinister. She jumped every time the wind whistled through the trees or the shutters rattled. "Come on, Jonathan," she grumbled, "answer the door!"

Several minutes passed. She banged on the door a few more times. The metallic clanging of the brass door knocker reminded her of a movie she'd seen once, where a bloodthirsty monster who'd escaped from prison dragged his heavy chains around as he stalked his chosen victims.

Jessica shook her head to clear away the nasty image. *But what if Katrina's murderer is still here, hanging around, watching for another victim?* she asked herself, trembling. She stood very still for a moment, listening to the sound of her own breathing.

Finally Jessica gave up and decided to leave Jonathan a note. Fumbling through her bag, she found a piece of scrap paper and a stubby pencil. *Tomorrow night, 6:30 P.M., Sunday dinner at my house*, she wrote, holding the paper flat against the rough surface of the porch railing.

And Jonathan, she added, grinning mischievously, *I expect us to continue where we left off last night.* She signed it with a flourish and stuck it in his mailbox.

Her body tingled with eagerness as she jogged back to the Jeep. *How am I supposed to wait until tomorrow night?* she wondered.

Chapter 5

Elizabeth peeked at the chicken bubbling in the oven. The cream sauce was laden with garlic and dill, creating an enticing aroma all through the house. The table had been set with the Wakefields' good china and silverware, at Jessica's insistence. The centerpiece, a shallow vase of white blossoms, was adorned on either side by clusters of white tapers ready to be lighted. *I'm surprised we didn't have to go out and buy finger bowls,* Elizabeth thought wryly.

It didn't matter to her how delicious the meal promised to be or how lovely everything looked. Elizabeth was too upset from all the horrible things going on to care. She still felt confused about Joey and Todd. And the thought of seeing Jonathan Cain again terrified her.

The doorbell rang. Elizabeth took a deep breath to brace herself. *I hope it's Joey,* she thought.

But when Elizabeth opened the door, it was Jonathan who stood on the front step. The sight of his pale skin and shimmering blue eyes made her skin crawl. "Oh, it's you," she grumbled.

His lips stretched into a tight, scary grin. "Yes, it is," he replied evenly. "It's nice to see you, Elizabeth."

The feeling isn't mutual, believe me, she silently retorted. She was gripped by an overwhelming feeling of dread. *I absolutely do not want him to enter my home!* she thought, trembling. The very idea of it made her want to scream. Resisting the urge to slam the door right in his face, she opened it wide and turned to walk away.

"Aren't you going to invite me in?" Jonathan drawled.

Elizabeth bristled at his arrogant tone. She looked over her shoulder and was surprised to see him hesitating in the doorway. She would have expected him to march right in, whether he was welcome or not. "Consider yourself invited," she said blandly.

Jonathan nodded solemnly and stepped into the foyer. Their eyes met briefly. Elizabeth gasped soundlessly as a fist of cold fear squeezed her throat.

❖   ❖   ❖

During dinner, Jonathan shoved his food around his plate, hoping no one would notice that he wasn't actually eating. When Mr. Wakefield passed him a basket of steaming rolls, Jonathan thanked him graciously and discreetly passed it on to Elizabeth's boyfriend without taking any for himself.

"I couldn't understand why the Nelsons wanted to paint their beautiful hardwood floors such a ghastly shade of green," Alice Wakefield was saying, her blue-green eyes twinkling with laughter. Jessica had told Jonathan that her mother was an interior decorator, but he hadn't expected her to be so lively and vivacious.

It was easy to see where Jessica had inherited her beauty. *And Elizabeth,* Jonathan conceded— although at that moment Jessica's twin was scowling across the table at him and hardly seemed attractive at all. He turned his attention away from her cold, hard gaze and focused on her mother's amusing story.

Mrs. Wakefield paused to take a bite of salad, her movements graceful and elegant. "I did manage to persuade them to lay down green carpet instead," she continued. "But then the Nelsons insisted on an orange velvet couch and orange brocade curtains." She shook her head, chuckling.

Across the table, Jessica flashed Jonathan a

flirty smile, then turned to her mother. "Sounds ugly, Mom."

"That's the very word that kept popping into my head—*ugly!*" her mother agreed. "And when Ms. Nelson turned to me and asked, 'What do you think of it, Alice?' I was stumped for an answer. Finally I blurted out that it reminded me of a pumpkin patch."

"You're lucky they didn't fire you," her husband teased.

"They were *pleased*," Mrs. Wakefield countered. "Apparently it was the look the Nelsons were going for. They explained that they'd made their fortune growing pumpkins in Washington State, and now that they've retired, they want to honor their former lifestyle."

Mr. Wakefield's lips twitched. "I guess you can take the Nelsons out of the pumpkin patch, but you can't take the pumpkin patch out of the Nelsons."

All the kids groaned, but Mrs. Wakefield gaped at her husband. "That's *exactly* what they said," she exclaimed.

Everyone at the table broke into peals of laughter. Jonathan felt honored to be included in the merriment. The warmth of the Wakefield family touched him deeply.

Family, he thought, testing the word in his

mind. A loving family was something he pined for, what he missed most of all. *And what I can never have again,* he reminded himself wistfully.

His dear grandmother would have been amazed if she could see the Wakefields' home—especially the spacious kitchen with its gleaming Spanish-tiled floor and modern appliances. Jonathan imagined her stocky form standing at the stove, cooking up a heaping platter of herring fresh from the Baltic Sea.

Jonathan remembered coming home to a warm fire in the hearth and the air filled with the tantalizing aroma of freshly baked *apfel kuchen,* their favorite apple and cinnamon pastry. Of course his little brother would try to steal an extra slice after dinner—which their grandmother had always pretended not to notice. His family's dinner table had been a place for warm, jovial gatherings, as it was for the Wakefield family.

Jonathan had often despaired of his family's lack of wealth. Too late he'd come to realize that although his home had been small and humble, it had been rich in love.

"So, Jonathan, when exactly are your parents coming back from Europe?" Elizabeth inquired, shattering his memory.

"In a few weeks," he responded evenly.

Her eyebrows rose, and she pursed her lips. "That long?"

Jonathan cleared his throat. "They had planned to come at the same time I did, but they were unexpectedly delayed because of their work."

From the corner of his eye, Jonathan saw Mrs. Wakefield give Elizabeth a cautioning look.

"I'm just curious," Elizabeth said defensively.

Her mother smiled indulgently. "Let the poor guy eat his dinner."

Jonathan glanced at his plate, and his stomach churned. He appreciated Mrs. Wakefield's concern, but the idea of putting the slimy chicken flesh into his mouth disgusted him. He looked up and shrugged. "I don't mind," he said.

Elizabeth immediately began firing more questions. "What do your parents do—for work, I mean?" she asked.

Jonathan suppressed a grin. Clearly Elizabeth had set herself up as his opponent, and he felt equal to the challenge. "They're musicologists," he told her. "They're currently doing research on a cache of musical scores that was recently discovered in Germany."

"Oh, really?" Elizabeth responded in a high pitch. "That's so interesting."

Across the table, Jessica gazed at Jonathan, her eyes filled with awe. He grinned, drawing a huge smile from her that seemed to light up her whole face. He noticed Joey trying to engage her sister in similar loving glances, but Elizabeth was too busy grilling Jonathan to notice.

"What kind of research are they doing?" she asked. Something about the fierce, stubborn expression on her face reminded Jonathan of a pit bull. He suspected that once she'd clamped her jaw down on someone, she'd never let go.

"Authenticity, first of all," he explained confidently.

"How do they determine that?" Elizabeth tore off a piece of bread and buttered it, as if the action could make her questions seem a bit more casual.

As Jonathan opened his mouth to answer, Mr. Wakefield chuckled. "Elizabeth, dinner is not the Spanish Inquisition," he pointed out gently.

Elizabeth blushed deep rose and finally shut up, like a muzzled beast. Jonathan silently cheered his small victory.

Jessica spirited Jonathan away to her father's den immediately after dinner. "I have a million new French verbs to memorize," she claimed. "Jonathan is going to help me—he's the top student in the class."

Elizabeth frowned as she watched them go. She was certain that Jessica had advertised the bit about Jonathan's class rank to influence their parents' opinion of him.

"That's OK, Liz," her mother said as Elizabeth

began stacking the dirty dishes. "Your father and I can clean up."

"Enjoy it while it lasts," her father remarked cheerfully.

Elizabeth stared at her parents, concerned about their good mood. She'd hoped that meeting Jonathan would have convinced them to keep him away from Jessica. But they didn't seem to mind in the least that their daughter was entertaining the creep at that very moment, behind a closed door. *Seems Jonathan has fooled them too*, she realized glumly.

Joey clasped her hand and led her into the living room. As soon as they were out of her parents' sight, he pulled her close for a big hug. "I've wanted to do that all evening," he whispered. "Let's go for a drive. I want to take you to Miller's Point, where we can be alone."

Elizabeth sighed. "I can't, remember? I'm grounded."

Joey rolled his eyes and chuckled. "I guess I forgot. What about sitting with me in the backyard by the pool? You *are* allowed outside the house, I hope?" he asked sarcastically.

She gave him a crooked smile. "Very funny."

He slung his arm across her shoulders. "Come on, Elizabeth. Just because you're grounded doesn't mean you have to lose your sense of humor."

Outside, Elizabeth and Joey sat side by side on

the edge of her family's in-ground swimming pool, dangling their feet in the cool blue water. The warm night air was lightly scented with the fragrance of roses and freshly mown grass.

Joey curved his arm around her waist. "Remember those nights at camp when we would sneak out of our cabins after lights-out and sit like this on the dock, dangling our feet into the lake?"

Elizabeth sighed at the memory. "The air smelled like campfires and pine trees."

He turned to her with a twinkle of laughter in his green eyes. "Let's do it tonight! I'll come by after your parents are asleep and we'll drive up to Miller's Point."

Elizabeth shook her head. "I couldn't do that."

"Why not?" he asked. "You never had a problem breaking the rules at camp."

"We're not at Camp Echo Mountain anymore, Joey," she pointed out. "This is the real world."

"And we don't have Nicole around to make you jealous," he added.

Elizabeth knew he was joking, but the remark stung. Nicole Banes, from New York, had instantly become Elizabeth's archenemy at camp. Ironically, Maria Slater, their common friend, had assumed that they would become great buddies on sight.

Eventually Elizabeth and Nicole had reached a truce, but not before they'd battled over everything, from who would use the only desk in their cabin all the way up to Maria's friendship—and Joey's love.

Would I have fallen so hard for Joey if Nicole hadn't tried to keep me away from him? Elizabeth asked herself. Although the question hurt, she searched her heart for the answer. But her feelings were a jumbled mess, as they had been since Joey had first come into her life.

"Have you heard from Nicole?" Elizabeth asked lamely, hoping to cover up her discomfort.

"Yes, she sent me a copy of a short story she'd published in a national literary magazine." He turned to Elizabeth with a saucy smile. "Are you jealous?"

"Of course," she teased. "What I wouldn't give to have one of *my* short stories published in a national magazine!"

Joey laughed good-naturedly. "Yeah, you're still the spunky girl I met at camp."

Am I? Elizabeth wondered. She wasn't too sure.

Joey tipped his head back to gaze at the sky. "We had more stars at Camp Echo Mountain. I'm surprised how few stars are visible out here."

Elizabeth remembered making a similar remark to Maria a short time back, but for some reason it bothered her to hear Joey say it. "But we have year-round sunshine and gorgeous beaches," she said defensively. "Not a bad trade, if you ask me."

"I agree," he whispered. "And this is where *you* are, which makes it the most beautiful place on earth. But right now I really miss Camp Echo Mountain. I want to pretend we're back in Montana, where you and I first met—and fell in love." He smiled gently. "You mean so much to me, Elizabeth."

Just looking into Joey's eyes used to make me feel a million different emotions at once, Elizabeth reflected longingly. She laced her fingers around his neck and threw herself into a passionate kiss, trying to recapture the romantic feelings she'd once had for him.

But Todd's face floated before her mind's eye, as she'd first seen it after she'd regained consciousness the night of Katrina's murder. His brown eyes had been filled with warmth and concern. *That scruffy beard he's trying to grow is so ridiculous,* Elizabeth thought, feeling a pang of tenderness. The more she tried to pull herself back to the present moment with Joey, the more clearly she remembered how comforted she'd felt in Todd's arms. Sighing wistfully, she pulled away from Joey.

He frowned. "What's the matter, Elizabeth?"

She glanced across the shadowy yard, hesitating. "I guess I'm just shaken up—about Friday night."

Joey pulled her close. "It must have been frightening for you," he whispered.

Elizabeth felt a twinge of guilt. *I'm not really lying,* she reasoned. She *was* upset about Friday night—but not just because of the murder.

What am I going to do about this dilemma? Elizabeth wondered. She was supposed to be the older, reliable, serious, cautious twin. *So what am I doing in love with two guys?*

Chapter 6

Jessica sat on Jonathan's lap and whispered her homework lesson into his ear. *"Je disparais,* I disappear, *tu disparais,* you disappear, *il ou elle disparaît,* he or she disappears." She leaned back and looked into his gorgeous blue eyes. "Lila says this French stuff is supposed to drive you crazy. Is it working?"

Jonathan curved his hand on the back of her neck and drew her closer.

"I guess it is," she murmured just before their lips met in a heart-stopping kiss. A kaleidoscope of delicious sensations raced through her. *Conjugating French verbs was never this much fun before,* Jessica thought.

After the kiss ended, she snuggled against Jonathan, feeling totally content. "I'm sure my parents like you," she told him. "But I knew they would," she added.

Jonathan absently brushed his fingers through her hair. "I really like them too," he murmured. "They remind me of my own parents."

"I suppose you miss them," she remarked. "I mean, after having to fend for yourself all this time. It must get tiring."

"I do miss them," he replied. "Sometimes we take people for granted." A faraway expression fluttered across his face. "When they're gone, you hate yourself because you never showed them how much you cared when you had the chance."

Jessica tightened her arms around him, trying to soothe the pain she heard in his voice.

He kissed her forehead. "You and I are alike in some ways," he said. "We grab every adventure that comes our way, but it's never enough. There's always something even more exciting and wonderful just up ahead, out of reach. We're terrified at what might happen if we stop chasing after the next thrill."

Jessica realized she was crying. "It's as though you can see into my soul." She brushed a tear from her cheek and rested her head on Jonathan's shoulder. "I feel like I've known you all my life," she sighed.

As they sat quietly Jessica felt an incredible sensation of peace flow through her body. It tickled something in her memory, but the images in her mind were vague. *A dream?* she wondered.

Jonathan cleared his throat. "Jessica, there are things you need to know about me. I'm not the person you think I am."

Jessica gazed up at him and felt the pull of his sexy eyes all the way down to her toes. "You're the person I love," she declared. "Nothing can change my feelings."

Jonathan brought her hand up to his lips. "I hope you mean that," he said, "because the truth is—"

His words were cut off by a discreet knock at the door of the den. Jessica giggled nervously as she jumped off Jonathan's lap and plopped down on the other end of the couch an instant before her father opened the door.

"It's after nine-thirty," Ned Wakefield announced. "You'd better get going, Jonathan, if you're going to make it home before the ten o'clock curfew."

Jonathan's eyes narrowed slightly. "Thanks for the warning," he replied politely. "I guess we lost track of the time."

"French verbs will do that," Jessica mumbled under her breath. Jonathan shot her a crooked grin, then rose to his feet.

Jessica felt a bittersweet ache in her heart as she walked him out to the driveway, where his motorcycle was parked. *I wish we never had to be away from each other,* she thought.

Jonathan hopped onto his bike and sighed. "I really did have a wonderful time."

Jessica absently ran her fingers over the clutch lever. "I'm glad," she said. "You'll come back soon, right?"

"Soon," he echoed. He leaned closer and kissed her. "We'll talk, Jessica." With that he took off, his bike roaring down the street.

Jessica stood in the driveway and listened to the fading sound. "I miss him already," she whispered.

A large crowd of mourners was gathered at Katrina's gravesite when Elizabeth, Jessica, and their parents arrived for the service the following day. The day was sunny and warm, which seemed odd to Elizabeth. She thought gray clouds and drizzle would have been more appropriate.

Penny Ayala had called that morning to tell Elizabeth that the *Oracle* staff was planning a special issue dedicated to Katrina's memory. Olivia Davidson, the arts editor, was going to take photographs at the service. Maria planned to submit a poem. Elizabeth had offered to write a "Personal Profiles" column about Katrina's life.

Although Amy's cousin had been in Sweet Valley for only a few weeks, a strong feeling of solidarity existed among the SVH students. It was as if one of their own had been taken away.

When Elizabeth reached the receiving line, she was enveloped in a huge hug by Dyan Sutton, Amy's mother. Elizabeth could see the devastating effect of the family's tragedy in her expression. As a television sportscaster, Mrs. Sutton usually presented a very polished, poised image. But that day Elizabeth saw only weariness and pain.

Amy's father smiled warmly and kissed Elizabeth's cheek, but his eyes were filled with agony and grief. He introduced Mimi Sutton, another cousin of Amy's, who attended Sweet Valley University.

When Elizabeth reached Amy, the two girls hugged each other tightly. They had been best friends a long time ago, until Amy's family had moved away from Sweet Valley. Although they hadn't resumed their close friendship after Amy's return, it didn't matter. At that moment their sadness bound them together.

"I'm so sorry, Amy," Elizabeth whispered, tears flowing unchecked down her cheeks.

Amy nodded and sniffled. "Thank you for trying to save her," she murmured. She introduced Elizabeth to Katrina's parents. The couple nodded, but they seemed to be staring through hollow eyes.

During the service, Elizabeth saw Todd standing with some of the guys a short distance away. The sunshine brought out the dark blue highlights of his newly black hair. The scraggly beard on his chin twitched as he swallowed, which he did a lot, as if he had a lump in his throat.

I wish Todd were beside me, she admitted to herself. She was relieved that Joey had declined when she'd asked him to come to the service.

"Although Katrina Sutton's life was tragically short," the minister was saying, "her memory lives in our hearts."

A few minutes later, a dark-haired Asian girl stood up to speak. "My name is Janet Chung, and I was Katrina's best friend in San Francisco." She told a few anecdotes of fun times they'd shared and read a poem that Katrina had written.

Standing next to Elizabeth, Jessica began to sob as Katrina's friend read the last line: "'And if I touch the heart of another, my walk on this earth is more precious than gold.'"

Elizabeth fumbled in her pocket for some tissues. She handed one to her twin, then wiped her own tears and blew her nose. From the corner of her eye, she caught a glimpse of Olivia as she discreetly snapped photographs for the *Oracle's* special issue.

Someone came up behind Elizabeth and touched her arm. She turned and saw Maria Slater standing there, her smooth ebony cheeks wet with tears. A meaningful look passed between them. Maria also had been a close friend of Amy's back in sixth grade. Elizabeth knew Katrina's death had affected her deeply.

Bruce Patman, Kirk Anderson, and Tim Nelson were standing directly behind Maria. All three of them appeared shaken. Elizabeth was about to turn around when she noticed Jonathan standing a few feet back, his features drawn into a smooth, masked expression.

Elizabeth's gaze hardened. *What is he thinking?* she wondered. A prickling sensation crawled up her back as she continued staring at him. His skin was as chalky as Katrina's when Elizabeth had tried to resuscitate her. *He's as pale as death,* she realized.

Elizabeth turned around and gulped in a deep breath. Despite the warm sunshine beaming down on her, she shivered.

With his eyes hidden behind dark sunglasses, Todd watched Elizabeth. Although she stood only a few yards away from him, the distance felt like miles. Everything about her fascinated him—the movement of her hand as she brushed away a tear, the flutter of her brown skirt in the wind, the glimmer of tears pooled in her gorgeous blue-green eyes. Todd's throat tightened. Elizabeth had never looked more beautiful to him. He wished he were standing with her, holding her hand.

Todd's mind pulled up images of their past,

71

moments when he'd thought Elizabeth would be with him forever. He recalled the first time he'd kissed her, after they'd finally unraveled Jessica's schemes to keep them apart. There was that crazy time when Elizabeth had joined her sister's cheerleading squad at the national competition. Desperate to see their girlfriends, Todd and some of the guys had sneaked into the all-girls compound dressed as female cheerleaders from Saskatchewan.

Todd remembered the quiet times: snuggled up with Elizabeth in her father's den, supposedly studying . . . long drives along the coastal highway . . . picnics at Secca Lake . . . parking at Miller's Point, steaming up the windows of his car. . . . His body ached, thinking of Elizabeth in his arms, the warm, sweet smell of her hair, her soft lips on his.

Todd groaned under his breath. The pain of being without Elizabeth ripped through his heart. After all they'd shared, he couldn't understand how he'd managed to lose her.

A veil of moisture stung his eyes. He still loved her. Being apart because of his pride didn't make any sense at all.

Katrina Sutton was only sixteen years old, Todd realized. *A girl our age is being buried! What if it had been Elizabeth who'd died at that party?* He gasped, as if the thought had kicked him in the stomach.

As a tear worked its way down his cheek, Elizabeth turned in his direction, and their eyes met. Todd swallowed against the thickening in his throat. Wordlessly he and Elizabeth moved toward each other. Todd clasped her hand, entwining their fingers. A feeling of rightness came over him, as if he could face anything with Elizabeth at his side.

For the rest of the service they stood close together, hand in hand. *No matter what it takes, I have to figure out a way to make things right between us,* he vowed.

Enid twisted a tissue in her fingers as she stood between Annie Whitman and Lynne Henry, two girls she'd recently become friends with after dumping Elizabeth Wakefield. Enid's new clique shared her attraction for Jonathan and had eagerly adopted his sexy, gothic style—which her *former* best friend, Elizabeth, was too narrow-minded and judgmental to understand.

Enid gritted her teeth as she glanced at Elizabeth and Todd holding hands. *I thought she was supposed to be going with Joey Mason,* Enid grumbled to herself. *It's not fair that someone like Elizabeth should have two guys falling at her feet!*

It wouldn't have mattered if a million guys were attracted to Enid; she wanted only one—Jonathan.

And thanks to the other *Wakefield twin, I've lost him,* she thought, sobbing.

She sniffled and wiped her tears, barely noticing that her tissue came away streaked with black eye makeup. What difference did it make if she looked like a complete mess? Jonathan—her soul mate—was in love with another.

Enid caught sight of Amy Sutton's tearstained face and blinked as she suddenly realized what was going on—and why. *Amy's cousin was murdered,* she reminded herself. But caught up as Enid was in her own pain, Katrina's death still didn't seem real to her.

After the burial service, the minister extended the Sutton family's invitation to a reception at their home. Enid lingered behind as the crowd dispersed. Although she'd told Lynne and Annie that she would meet them at Amy's house, she made no move to follow.

After everyone else had gone, Enid sat on the grassy ground and stared at the fresh grave. All the flower arrangements had been piled over the dirt, and the air was filled with the scent of lilies and chrysanthemums.

She traced the petals of a large white blossom with her black fingernail. "I'm sorry I wasn't crying for you, Katrina," she whispered. "To tell you the truth, I wasn't even thinking about you. But I should have been. It's just that my life is such a big mess."

Enid wiped her hand across her cheek. "I'm not sure when all the bad stuff began," she continued. "Ever since Maria Slater moved back to Sweet Valley, Elizabeth's been ignoring me. Then I fell in love with Jonathan—I mean, fell *really* hard. And I thought he loved me too. I can still remember the day I showed up at school with a hickey on my neck. It was so great!"

Enid smiled for an instant, then fresh tears flooded her eyes. "It wasn't fair, Katrina. Why would he act so loving toward me, then ditch me for Jessica?"

Enid continued unburdening herself, absently pulling up tufts of grass as she spoke. A sense of peace began to seep into her weary body. The afternoon sunshine was warm and soothing on her skin. All around her, the cemetery lawns were green and lush. But there was more—she also felt an odd kinship with Katrina, as if the girl's death held a lesson for Enid's own life.

"Poor Katrina," she whispered. "I'm really sorry you're gone."

"I wish Enid had come to the reception," Elizabeth told Maria as the two girls left the Suttons' home. Hundreds of mourners had crowded into the lovely mission-style house to pay their respects to the Sutton family. The tree-lined street was crowded with parked cars for several blocks. Maria had elected to leave her Mercedes at Elizabeth's house, a short distance away.

"I don't know Enid very well," Maria admitted. "But I still say she's acting a lot like Nicole did at camp."

Elizabeth shook her head. "Nicole was jealous because you and I were friends. Enid isn't like that."

"Are you sure?" Maria asked.

"Absolutely sure," Elizabeth replied without hesitation. She absently stepped across a stream of soapy water that flowed down a driveway where a man was washing a car. "I remember when Amy moved back to Sweet Valley," Elizabeth explained. "I tried so hard to be her friend, I wound up treating Enid badly—breaking plans all over the place without calling her—and she was totally understanding."

A ball bounced into their path. Maria caught it and tossed it back to the group of young boys playing in a front yard across the street. "You shouldn't blame yourself for Enid's problems, Liz."

"I don't, not really," Elizabeth said. "But I'm afraid for her. Enid has always been there for me when I needed her. Now that she needs me, I've let her down." A tear slipped onto Elizabeth's cheek. "I was too caught up in my own problems to pay attention to hers. And I *do* blame myself for that," she admitted.

"The situation isn't hopeless yet," Maria assured her. "Remember how terrible it got between you and Nicole at camp? She stole your play, for heaven's sake! But in the end everything worked out. By the way, did you know she sold a short story to a national magazine?"

Elizabeth nodded. "Joey told me last night."

"And don't worry, I'm sure she didn't steal it," Maria said breezily. "I've read it. It's about her cousin Albert, and no one else in the world could have written it."

Elizabeth's lips twitched. The idea *had* crossed her mind. "I just hope Enid and I can put our friendship back together when this is all over," she murmured. "I'm terribly worried about her."

The sky was streaked with purple and red as a silent figure moved across the graveyard. The lengthening shadows of the headstones on the cool grass were a welcome sight. With the setting of the hot sun, he felt his strength returning.

And his need . . .

His mind raged with hunger. He groaned softly, his fists clenched. How he hated the gnawing ache that burned in his gut, the driving need that screamed to be satisfied!

77

Some distance away, he saw a girl sitting alone by a freshly dug grave. The fading light cast a bluish orange glow over her bare arms. A breeze fluttered through her jet black hair, as if to entice him.

I can't . . . I won't, he vowed, trying to fight his blazing desire.

But his body cried out for relief. *It will be night soon,* he thought eagerly. Unable to stop himself, he crept toward her.

Enid shivered as a cool breeze chilled her skin. She'd been unaware of how much time had passed and was surprised to find that the evening had grown dark around her. *There's a serial killer on the loose, and I'm sitting alone in a dark graveyard!* she realized, terrified.

She heard a soft rustling sound behind her and jumped, her heart in her throat. Trembling, she looked around but saw no one. *I'm just being paranoid,* she chided herself.

Suddenly a pair of strong hands grabbed her from behind, squeezing her neck.

Chapter 7

"Katrina was planning to go to Sweet Valley University," Amy told her friends. "We were going to be roommates."

Lila and Jessica exchanged sorrowful glances. The three of them were in Amy's room, sitting together on her bed. "We're all so sorry this happened," Lila said softly.

Amy made a sound that was half cry and half laugh. "I miss her so much!" she sobbed.

Jessica draped her arm around Amy's shoulders. "I know you do."

"I wish I'd never talked her into coming to Sweet Valley," Amy declared, her voice shaking. She jumped up and began pacing across her spacious room. "I'll tell you this: The police had better find the person who killed my cousin, because I'm not going to rest until they do. And if they can't, I'll find the killer myself."

She banged her fist on top of her yellow dresser, her slate gray eyes flashing. "If it takes the rest of my life, I swear I'll find Katrina's murderer! Even if I have to do it all alone."

"But you're not alone," Lila insisted as she and Jessica rushed over to Amy.

"She's right," Jessica agreed. "We're your friends and you can always count on us. We'll help you in any way we can. That's a promise," she added.

Jonathan saw Enid's body lying on the ground. Her skin was deathly pale, but when he put his fingers to her throat, he felt a weak pulse. His face contorted at the sight of the darkening bruises around her neck.

He buried his head in his hands, aghast. *I came here to find peace, but I've brought Sweet Valley nothing but heartache. And now this!* He cursed himself, thinking of how badly he'd treated Enid. *I've repaid her kindness with horror and pain,* he admitted harshly.

In that moment Jonathan resolved to do what was right. *There's a first time for everything,* he thought. He gently lifted Enid up in his arms and carried her to his motorcycle. Her eyes fluttered open for a moment, gazing at him with a bewildered, frightened look.

"Don't worry," he whispered. "I'm getting you help."

The ringing of the telephone crashed through Elizabeth's fitful dream the following morning. Squeezing her eyes shut, she snuggled under the covers and tried to block out the irritating sound. It didn't work; the noise still reached her ears.

Elizabeth opened her eyes and groaned. Her room was dark and shadowy in the pale dawn light. "It's too early for this," she whined as she grabbed the phone.

"Elizabeth?" Ms. Rollins asked in a shaky voice.

Suddenly alert, Elizabeth sat up and braced herself for what she was sure was bad news. "What's wrong?"

"I'm calling from the hospital," Ms. Rollins told her. "Enid was attacked last night. She's in intensive care right now, in critical condition. If it hadn't been for one of the guys from school finding her and rushing her to the emergency room . . . I don't want to think what might have happened."

Elizabeth gulped, her whole body frozen in shock. "Will she be OK?"

"I hope so." There was a pause on the line. "Elizabeth, I know things haven't been the same between you two lately, but—"

Elizabeth broke into tears. "Enid is still my best friend!" she cried, swinging her legs over the side of her bed. "I'm coming to the hospital right now. I'll be there in a few minutes."

After she hung up, Elizabeth bolted into action. She tugged on her jeans, pulled a gray sweatshirt over her head, and pushed her feet into a pair of canvas sandals. She left a note on the kitchen table for her parents and Jessica, then rushed outside to the Jeep.

Elizabeth recalled the image of Katrina's lifeless body lying on Jonathan's living room floor. *Please don't die, Enid!* she silently pleaded, choking back a sob as she took off for Joshua Fowler Memorial Hospital.

Jessica had been counting on Lila to help take her mind off the terrible news of Enid's attack, but when she hopped into her friend's Triumph convertible later that morning, Lila's expression was depressingly somber.

"Have you heard anything more about Enid?" Lila asked. Jessica had filled her in earlier when she'd called to arrange the ride to school.

"She's still in critical condition." Jessica sighed.

"I know I've never been too crazy about Enid, but still . . ."

"I understand what you mean," Lila said. "Right now it doesn't matter that the girl has no fashion sense or style whatsoever. I feel really sorry for her anyway."

Both girls fell silent. Jessica longed for anything that could take her mind off the horror happening around her. "Elizabeth and Joey seem to be getting serious," she remarked, knowing Lila's penchant for gossip. "How long do you think it'll take Todd to start dating someone else?"

Lila shrugged but said nothing.

Jessica slumped down in the seat and glanced at the passing scenery. *The one time I was actually looking forward to Lila's nonstop chatter, she decides to shut up,* she thought. *Even listening to her boasting about Bo would be better than this.*

For weeks Lila had been driving everyone crazy with her constant babbling about Beauregard "Bo" Creighton III, her rich boyfriend in Washington, D.C. Whenever anyone mentioned a subject remotely connected with him, Lila would plunge into a marathon session of Bo this and Bo that, rattling off French phrases in an effort to sound sophisticated.

"So tell me, Lila. Have you heard from Bo lately?" Jessica asked pointedly.

Lila's nodded. "We talked last night."

"In French?" she teased.

Lila shook her head without even cracking a smile.

That's it? Jessica thought, staring at her in astonishment. *If Lila's too upset to gush about Bo, then the situation is truly hopeless.*

School was equally grim. Everyone was still shaken by Katrina's death, and before the end of first period, news of Enid's attack had spread throughout the building, adding to the horror.

Ms. McLean, the school psychologist, took over Jessica's English class to speak with the students about the recent violence in Sweet Valley. "We're expanding the hours of the counseling center for the next two weeks," she explained just before the period ended. "And I invite each and every one of you to make an appointment if you continue to feel troubled about what has happened."

"Who doesn't feel troubled?" Lila mumbled as she and Jessica squeezed through the hall after class. "Caroline Pearce told me that when Mrs. Green, the guidance counselor, visited her first-period class to do this, three of the girls broke down hysterically and had to leave."

Jessica followed her to the girls' room and plopped her bag down in front of a mirror.

"Anyway," Lila continued, "I could have done without the impromptu group therapy session. I don't know about you, but now I'm more depressed than ever."

Jessica pulled out her hairbrush. "I feel exactly the same. And when I glanced at the absentee list on Mr. Collins's desk, Jonathan's name was on it."

Lila rolled her eyes. "Now there's a *real* tragedy," she said sarcastically.

Jessica's hand paused in midair, gripping the handle of her hairbrush. "What's *that* supposed to mean?"

"It was a joke, Jess," Lila replied. "I'm just trying to loosen things up. I think right now I'd even let you poke fun at Bo."

Jessica smiled, instantly contrite. "Everything is so awful. Lately I can't even think straight!" She turned back to her reflection and frowned. Her makeup was perfect. She wore a sleeveless yellow top that brought out the golden highlights in her hair. Her slim black jeans showed off her perfect, athletic figure. But something was wrong.

Jessica tilted her head and pursed her lips. "Why do I feel so ugly today?" she asked aloud.

Lila gave her a playful shove. "Because you are."

Jessica chuckled halfheartedly and shoved her back. "Come on, Lila. Let's hurry up and get in the lunch line before they run out of institutional slop."

Lila raised her fist and slung her other arm over Jessica's shoulders. "*Place aux dames!*"

"Did you just swear?" Jessica asked, laughing.

Lila glared at her. "No, you silly girl. It means 'make way for the ladies.'"

"You're so obnoxious," Jessica teased. "I can't believe how much I've missed that."

Jessica's halfway good mood lasted nearly five minutes. In the cafeteria, a bunch of kids were gathered around Bruce. He waved Jessica and Lila over to his table. "Have you heard anything more about Enid?" he asked.

"Just that she's in critical condition," Jessica answered. "Elizabeth is at the hospital."

"And what are the police doing about it?" he asked loudly. "I'll bet they haven't got a single lead on this maniacal murderer."

"Do they believe Enid was attacked by the same guy who killed Katrina?" Todd asked.

Jessica shook her head. "I don't know."

"Who else could it be?" Bruce demanded. "It was the same guy, all right!" A murmur of agreement buzzed through the group.

"If it was, he's going to pay!" Amy shouted, her gray eyes simmering with rage.

"It does seem unlikely that a town the size

of Sweet Valley would have two deranged killers," Winston chimed in. "Now, take a city like L.A.—"

Everyone glared at him. Winston ducked his head sheepishly and raised his hands in surrender. "OK, I'll shut up."

"This isn't a joke," Amy snapped.

"I'll say it isn't," Lila agreed. "I'm sick of sitting around the house every night, wondering who'll die next."

Kirk Anderson threw his half-eaten sandwich on his tray. "I haven't been able to sleep since the night of Jonathan's party," he admitted. "And what good is that stupid curfew? They're telling us to stay home and to avoid hanging out by ourselves. But Amy's cousin was murdered *inside* Jonathan's house, right in the middle of a crowd."

Tim Nelson laughed derisively. "And the police want everyone to stay *calm*."

Bruce stood up and slapped his hands on the table. "Since the police are doing such a bad job of catching the killer, I say it's up to us to take matters into our own hands," he declared.

"I agree," Amy said emphatically.

The crowd fell silent for a moment. Then Todd spoke up. "I think I do too. Something has to be done. We can't go on like this." A murmur of consent spread through the group.

"We'll show that homicidal maniac that he can't get away with killing off Sweet Valley kids!" Aaron Dallas boasted.

"Let's show the police how it's done!" Blubber Johnson said, banging his heavy fist on the table. With a loud clatter, several trays bounced.

A chant rose from the group, which seemed to be rapidly turning into a mob. "Kill the killer, kill the killer . . ."

Seeing the rage on everyone's face, Jessica felt a tremor of fear. It seemed as if things were about to become even more out of control than they already were. *I wish Jonathan were here today,* she thought, longing for him. *He'd know just how to handle this angry mob.*

Elizabeth leaned forward in an orange plastic chair, bracing her elbows on her knees. She hadn't left Enid's side since she first arrived that morning. Staring at her friend lying still in the hospital bed, Elizabeth's heart felt twisted in knots.

Enid's mother sat on the other side of the bed, her expression grim. A monitor beeped along with Enid's heartbeat; a series of tubes and bottles ran to and from her battered body.

The hours dragged by slowly. Elizabeth felt overwhelmed by fear and regret. *Please wake up,*

Enid, she silently pleaded. She thought back to her conversation with Maria after Amy's funeral. *I do blame myself for this,* Elizabeth admitted, choking back a sob. If only she hadn't been so caught up with her own life.

Elizabeth didn't know what she'd do without Enid's constant, loyal friendship. They'd had so much fun together, doing simple things like baking cookies on a Saturday afternoon or going to see old movies at the Plaza. Elizabeth remembered the horrible night that Todd had been arrested, when the Sweet Valley guys had become embroiled in a gang war with the guys from Palisades High. Enid had been the one person she could turn to in the midst of all that craziness.

A nurse breezed into the tiny room, her soft-soled shoes barely making a sound. When she'd finished checking Enid's blood pressure and respiration rate, Elizabeth and Ms. Rollins both looked at her hopefully.

"No change," the nurse told them.

Elizabeth closed her eyes, tears slipping down her cheeks. *You have to make it, Enid,* she thought. *I refuse to let you die!*

Jonathan was absent from school for the next few days. Jessica grew frantic with worry. She tried calling him repeatedly and left dozens of messages in his mailbox.

By Friday she felt as if she were ready to explode like a volcano. Then she walked into her last-period French class and her jaw dropped. Jonathan was sitting in his usual seat, looking at her with a casual expression on his face.

Jessica didn't know whether to throw herself into his arms or throw her books at his head. She drifted to the seat next to him, her mind whirling in a million directions. She was barely aware that Ms. Dalton walked to the head of the class and started the lesson.

Clenching her teeth, Jessica ripped out a sheet of notebook paper. *Where have you been?* she wrote in large, bold letters. She tossed the note onto Jonathan's desk and shot him a challenging look.

Before she and Jonathan had gotten together, Jessica had passed him many notes, only to watch him crumple them up and toss them on the floor. *We'd better not be back to that little game,* she thought impatiently. After all they'd shared, Jonathan owed her an explanation. *I'm his girlfriend and I have a right to know where he's been,* she told herself.

Finally he picked up the note. Jessica's heart skipped a beat as she watched his long, elegant fingers unfold it. No matter what, she knew she couldn't stay angry at him for very long. She loved him so much, her heart ached.

Her gaze moved to the ornate ring he wore on his right hand. It was carved of wood and inlaid with silver and onyx. The first time she'd noticed it, Jessica had vowed that Jonathan would give it to her someday. *Someday soon*, she promised herself now.

Jonathan wrote something on the bottom of her note and passed it back to her. Jessica's heart pounded as she quickly opened it and read his response: *Can I come to your house tomorrow?*

Jessica bit her bottom lip to stifle a wild cheer. *An entire Saturday with Jonathan*, she thought, utterly delighted. For the rest of the period, she drew hearts all over her notebook with pink marker and wrote *Yes!* in each one.

Although it occurred to her that Jonathan hadn't answered her question, Jessica was too excited to care.

Saturday morning, Elizabeth arrived at Joshua Fowler Memorial Hospital shortly after sunrise. As she reached her friend's room, she heard Ms. Rollins asking Enid a question about school.

Elizabeth uttered a strangled cry of joy as she rushed into the room. But Enid's eyes were still closed, the tubes and machines still in place.

Elizabeth frowned and gazed questioningly at Ms. Rollins.

Enid's mother shook her head sadly. "There hasn't been any change in her condition," she murmured. "But the doctor said that hearing a friendly voice may help her regain consciousness."

"It's worth a try," Elizabeth agreed as she crossed the room to sit in the other chair. She'd sat in the same spot every morning before school and every afternoon until just before dark.

Ms. Rollins talked to Enid about funny things that had happened when she was a baby. Then Elizabeth took over, making plans for when Enid recovered.

"*Key Largo* starts next week at the Plaza," Elizabeth told Enid, doing her best to sound cheerful. "Humphrey Bogart is great in all his movies, but the ones where he costars with Lauren Bacall are the best. Maybe it's because there was all that chemistry—"

Suddenly Enid began to stir. Elizabeth held her breath and frantically waved Ms. Rollins over to the bed. A soft, moaning sound emerged from Enid's mouth.

With tears streaming down her face, Ms. Rollins clasped her daughter's hand. "Enid, honey?"

Enid's eyes fluttered open, and she whispered a

single word: "Jonathan." Then she slipped back into unconsciousness.

Elizabeth's heart plunged. *Jonathan?* she repeated to herself. *I knew it!* With a rising flood of panic, she jumped to her feet. "I have to leave now," she announced. "I'll be back as soon as I can." Without waiting for Ms. Rollins to respond, Elizabeth rushed out of the room.

Chapter 8

Jessica paced across the kitchen as far as the telephone cord would reach. "Come on, Jonathan, answer!" she barked into the phone. They were supposed to spend the entire day together, but she hadn't heard from him yet and hadn't been able to reach him.

The front door suddenly crashed open and Elizabeth rushed into the kitchen. Without a word, she disconnected the call.

Jessica scowled at her. "What did you do that for?"

"Sit down," Elizabeth said breathlessly. "I have to tell you something."

Annoyed, Jessica slammed down the phone and plunked herself into a chair across from her twin. "Sometimes, Elizabeth, you can be the most infuriating, rude, obnoxious—"

"Be quiet and listen," Elizabeth ordered.

Jessica's mouth snapped shut—not because of Elizabeth's high-handed manner, but because of the strange look on her face. "What happened, Liz?" Jessica asked, suddenly frightened. "Is it Enid? Did she—?" Jessica couldn't make herself say the rest of the sentence aloud, but she thought it: *Did she die?*

Elizabeth shook her head. "It's Jonathan. I'm almost positive that he's somehow involved in the killings. At the very least, he's the one who attacked Enid."

Jessica reeled back, as if she'd been struck. "Have you gone completely nuts?" she cried.

"Enid woke up briefly just now and said Jonathan's name," Elizabeth explained. "I think she was trying to tell us—"

Jessica jumped up, knocking over her chair. She set it right with a firm thud and glared at her twin. "How dare you!" she growled. "Enid Rollins mumbles *my* boyfriend's name, and you automatically assume he's a serial killer?"

"I know it's hard to believe something so terrible about a guy you care for," Elizabeth said in a sickeningly sweet, understanding-big-sister tone that made Jessica's blood boil.

"Who do you think you are, making up these horrible accusations about Jonathan?" Jessica slammed her fist on the table. "You're worse than

Caroline Pearce and Lila and all the other gossips in Sweet Valley High combined!"

"Will you please just keep an open mind and let me explain?" Elizabeth pleaded.

"No!" Jessica shot back hotly. "I'm sick of hearing you say terrible things about the guy I love." She whirled around and stormed out of the kitchen.

"Come back here, Jess. We're not finished," Elizabeth called.

"Oh, yes we *are*," Jessica shouted as she ran upstairs. Elizabeth followed close behind, but Jessica ducked into her bedroom and slammed the door in her sister's face.

Elizabeth banged on the door. "Let me in, Jess. We have to talk about this."

"Go away!" Jessica hollered. "I never want to speak to you again!"

"That's all Enid said? 'Jonathan'?" Maria asked the following day, after Elizabeth told her what had happened at the hospital.

Elizabeth nodded as she paced around Maria's bedroom. "You know what bothers me most about Jonathan?" She tapped her fingers against her lips as she gathered her thoughts into words. "Most people have signs that tell you who they really are."

Maria frowned, obviously confused.

"Take this bedroom, for instance," Elizabeth

began, sweeping her arm in an arc. "Bright blue wallpaper, sunny yellow curtains, movie posters on the wall, a picture of Maya Angelou on the closet door, a computer . . ." Elizabeth checked out the stuff on top of Maria's dresser. "Tons of makeup, a photograph of you and your sister in a silver frame, used makeup sponges . . ."

"Enough, Liz," Maria complained. "What's your point?"

Elizabeth raised her eyebrows. "Don't you see? Even if I didn't know you, I could guess the sort of person whose room this is. But Jonathan keeps himself completely hidden behind a mask. There *has* to be a reason why."

Maria leaned back in her cushioned armchair, which was covered in the same yellow fabric the curtains were made from. "Could it be that you're just groping for a quick answer to all these horrible murders?" she suggested. "It would be a perfectly understandable reaction if you were."

"Absolutely not," Elizabeth insisted. "There have been three murders since Jonathan arrived in Sweet Valley, each committed the same way—by draining the victim's blood. Jessica's kitten was killed like that too. Admit it, Maria—doesn't it seem a bit suspicious to you?"

Maria shrugged. "Circumstantial evidence, and you know it."

Elizabeth threw up her hands in defeat. "No one else believes me either."

"That's not what I'm saying, Liz," Maria countered. "I agree that Jonathan is a creepy, slimy weirdo who seems capable of committing any number of gruesome crimes. But I wish we had more information about him, some concrete facts to back up our hunches."

Elizabeth plopped down on the edge of Maria's bed. "The cops aren't even checking him out—which is totally incredible, considering that Katrina was murdered right in his living room." Elizabeth shook her head. "Everyone thinks he's wonderful, sophisticated, and brilliant. But when he was telling me about his parents at dinner last Sunday, I knew he was lying. I could see it in his eyes." She shuddered, remembering those feverish blue eyes boring into her like lasers.

"Unfortunately, that's not enough," Maria pointed out. "Lying eyes aren't admissible evidence." She snorted. "I could just imagine what Jessica would do if she heard what you're saying about her true love."

"Jessica thinks I've gone completely nuts," Elizabeth admitted.

Maria gaped at her. "You actually told her all of this?"

Elizabeth shrugged and looked away. "As much as I could before she ran into her room and slammed the door in my face."

Maria whistled. "You're one brave woman, Wakefield."

"I had to try," Elizabeth responded. "But you're right—we need facts to back up our suspicions."

"Too bad we don't know a good private investigator," Maria remarked. "Someone to go sleuthing through Jonathan Cain's murky background."

Elizabeth's eyes widened as a brilliant scheme popped into her head. "Yes!" She snapped her fingers and turned to Maria. "I have an idea. . . ."

Enid moved through a thick, steamy haze. Chattering voices surrounded her—strange conversations she couldn't understand. Her feet made a crunching sound with each step she took.

The fog began to clear. Enid watched herself walking along a crowded cobblestone street. Church bells rang in the distance. Horse-drawn carriages rattled by, and the air was heavy with the odor of horse manure. Enid noticed several women holding dainty lace handkerchiefs to their noses.

As she approached the churchyard she saw a wagon with passengers pulling up just ahead of her. Something about it caught her eye. She held her breath, watching.

A beautiful young man was the first to jump down from the wagon. There was something com-

pelling about him . . . . Enid's heart leaped in her chest. It was Jonathan.

He helped an elderly woman climb down. Then a young boy hopped out, followed by a pleasant-looking couple. The last person to step down was a lovely girl, just a few years older than Jonathan.

Enid knew that she was seeing Jonathan's family. She could feel the love they had for one another. Surrounded by them, Jonathan seemed younger, less intense. The dark, bleak look was absent from his eyes. Enid wept for him, for the happiness he'd once had.

Suddenly, from the corner of her eye, Enid saw an elegant carriage approaching. Its passenger was a woman dressed in a black chiffon gown, with a black veil over her face. She had the graceful manner of a lady, but there was something in her eyes . . . a strange, evil glint.

The woman was staring right at Jonathan, but he was too involved with his family to notice her. Enid tried to scream a warning to him, but no sound came out of her mouth.

The next thing Enid saw was a long black hole in the ground. She crouched down and peered into it, but it was too dark to see. Then she heard Jonathan moaning with horror.

And then nothing.

"This is absolutely crazy," Maria said to Elizabeth

as they crept toward Jonathan's crumbling mansion Monday evening. "I can't believe we're doing this."

Neither can I, Elizabeth agreed silently as she stared up at the house. Several gables and turrets rose haphazardly from the roof, casting eerie shadows in the moonlight. A gnarled tree grew in the front yard, and its long, spindly branches scratched against an upstairs window, setting Elizabeth's teeth on edge.

Although Elizabeth was still grounded at night, she'd told her parents that she needed a book from the library for a school assignment. She felt guilty about the lie, but finding out about Jonathan was crucial. The safety of Sweet Valley was at stake, not to mention that of her own twin.

When they reached the front porch, Maria hesitated, her brown eyes wide and luminous. "Are you sure he's seeing Jessica tonight?"

"Yes, according to the gossip at school today," Elizabeth whispered. "Jessica still isn't speaking to me."

"You don't think Jonathan would do something horrible to us if he caught us here, do you?"

Elizabeth glared at her. "I think he's a *murderer,* Maria, not a gentleman. And will you stop talking about getting caught? You're turning me into a nervous wreck."

Maria ducked her head. "Sorry. But I'm really scared, Liz."

Elizabeth nodded in empathy but urged her forward.

Starting with the front door and windows, they circled the entire house in search of a way inside, but everything on the first floor was locked tight.

"I don't think we should try climbing up to the higher windows," Elizabeth remarked. "The roof looks like it's ready to cave in." She and Maria were standing at the steps of the back porch, which was in worse shape than the front porch.

"I guess we can't get in, then," Maria said with a note of relief in her voice.

"We have to," Elizabeth insisted. She shone her flashlight beam along the edges of the back door. "There has to be a way. Maybe I can pick the lock."

Maria shot her a withering look.

Undaunted, Elizabeth stepped across the porch, carefully avoiding the gaping holes where the wood had completely rotted away. She crouched down in front of the back door, her eyes level with the lock, and pulled a baby-doll barrette out of her hair. "This always works in the movies, at least with a hairpin."

Maria snorted. "I hate to shock you, Elizabeth, but as a former Hollywood actress, I feel obligated to tell you this: The movies are make-believe."

"No kidding," Elizabeth responded blandly. She pushed the metal prong of the barrette into the keyhole and twisted it. "I can feel the latch . . . darn!"

"What happened?" Maria asked.

"I dropped the barrette. Hold on."

Maria came up behind her. "It's getting late, Liz. You're never going to get that door unlocked."

"You're right." With a pang of desperation, Elizabeth slammed the butt of her flashlight against the glass pane. The sound of shattering glass seemed to echo in the silence of the night.

"Elizabeth!" Maria gasped. "I can't believe you did that."

"Neither can I," Elizabeth replied breathlessly. Careful to avoid the sharp edges, she reached through the jagged hole and unlocked the door.

"So where are you, Jonathan?" Jessica chanted under her breath as she paced across the living room. He was supposed to have come by hours earlier, but so far there hadn't been any sign of him.

Jessica had forgiven him for standing her up on Saturday and for not calling her all weekend. But this time he'd gone too far. *I can't believe I'm being stood up again!* she fumed silently.

She pushed aside the front curtain and stared out the window. Mrs. Beckwith from next door drove by in her yellow Buick. Mr. Kilgartens, another neighbor, was walking his dog. There was no sign of a Harley-Davidson motorcycle.

Tears of frustration pooled in Jessica's eyes. *I have to see Jonathan,* her mind screamed. Her whole body yearned for him. If he wasn't going to come to her, she'd have to go looking for him.

But her parents were keeping a close watch on her. She could hear their voices in the kitchen at that very moment. There was no way she could sneak out of the house. *Of course, goody-two-shoes Elizabeth managed to get permission to go to the library,* Jessica thought with a flash of resentment.

Wait a minute, she thought excitedly. *The library! They'll have to let me go too.* Although her parents were much too strict and overly protective most of the time, they could always be counted on to be fair.

Jessica ran upstairs to her room and grabbed her backpack, which was empty. Putting on her sweetest, most innocent smile, she breezed into the kitchen. "I just remembered I need a book from the library for my homework," she announced.

Her parents turned to her with matching skeptical looks. "What book is it that you need?" her mother asked pointedly.

"It's the book we're doing in English," Jessica replied. "I left my copy in school and have to read it for tomorrow's class. And write a report," she added.

"*What* book?" her mother asked again.

"Oh, you mean the title?" Jessica inhaled deeply and struggled to remember what they were actually reading in her English class. "I know—'The Fall of the House of Usher,' by Edgar Allan Poe."

Her father grinned. "You're in luck, Jessica. There's a short-story anthology in the bookcase in the den, and I'm almost positive 'The Fall of the House of Usher' is in it."

Jessica blinked, then regained her poise. "Oh, wait—that's not right. We're doing 'The Raven.'"

"Nice try, Jess," her mother quipped.

Furious, Jessica stomped upstairs to her room, slammed the door, and flopped down on her bed. A flood of tears seeped into her pillow as waves of anger, desperation, and longing crashed over her. *My life is a shambles,* she thought.

Elizabeth's heart pounded like a kettledrum against her chest as she and Maria stalked through the dark interior of Jonathan's house. Even with the light of their flashlights, it felt as if they were moving through a black tunnel. As they entered the shadowy living room something crashed against the wall. Elizabeth and Maria grabbed each other, both of them trembling.

After a few horrifying seconds, Elizabeth realized what had made the noise. With a sigh she said, "It was just a loose shutter outside the window."

Maria exhaled a shaky breath. "Let's get this over with as quickly as possible."

"I agree," Elizabeth muttered, terrified. She kept remembering when she and Todd had searched in the dark for the fuse box during Jonathan's party—the night of Katrina's murder. "Let's start upstairs," she suggested, shining her flashlight on the circular staircase in the corner of the room.

Maria hesitated. "I don't know . . ."

"Come on," Elizabeth urged. As she gingerly led the way to the stairs, a floorboard creaked. Elizabeth jumped, her heart in her throat. "This place is so creepy!" she whimpered.

"Brilliant, Liz. What was your first clue?" Maria responded tersely.

Upstairs, they found themselves in a dark, narrow hall with several closed doors on either side. The floor was covered with a faded Persian carpet, and dusty old paintings hung crookedly on the wall.

The first door opened into an ominous, dark room with boarded-up windows. The only furnishings were a tall standing mirror and a giant armoire. The room across the hall was completely bare, with a huge hole in the floor. They were about to leave when something scratched at the window. Elizabeth and Maria shrieked and grabbed each other again. After a moment Maria laughed uncertainly. "It's only a branch from that ugly tree next to the house," she remarked.

Elizabeth ventured a glance and saw that Maria was right. In the moonlight, the branches looked like the silvery talons of a huge monster.

The next room had no windows at all. Elizabeth and Maria slowly moved their flashlight beams around the dark space, illuminating an oak four-poster bed and a rickety old desk. Against the wall was a low table with an oil lamp and matches on it. A huge antique chest stood at the foot of the bed, its length equal to the width of the bed frame.

Elizabeth frowned. "Do you suppose Jonathan sleeps in this room?"

"How should I know?" Maria whispered. "If this were my house, I'd sleep in a motel."

After searching the remaining rooms off the upstairs hall, the girls went back downstairs and checked out the kitchen, dining room, and living room. "I wonder who that is," Maria said, shining her flashlight on the portrait that hung over the fireplace.

The man in the painting was dressed in the elaborate style of the 1700s, in a black riding jacket with a turned-up collar and an ivory ascot at his throat. His dark hair was tied back in a Thomas Jefferson–style ponytail.

"I noticed that painting during the party,"

Elizabeth said. "There's something weird about it."

"It looks a lot like Jonathan," Maria remarked, "especially the eyes. It's spooky how they seem to be watching us."

Elizabeth nodded. "You're right. Maybe that's what was bothering me."

"It could be one of Jonathan's ancestors," Maria said.

The sound of an approaching car startled them. Thinking fast, Elizabeth pulled Maria into the dark, dusty space under the staircase. They held their breath as the beam of the car's headlights shone through the windows, sweeping across the room like a searchlight. Finally the car passed, the noise of its engine drifting away.

"This is so ridiculous," Elizabeth muttered, wiping cobwebs off her mouth as she crawled out of their hiding place.

"I want to get out of here," Maria whined.

"We should check the rest of the rooms on this floor," Elizabeth countered. "But maybe it would be best if you went outside and kept watch."

Maria hesitated. "I don't want to leave you in here alone."

"I'll be all right," Elizabeth assured her. "If anyone comes, tap on the side window and run to the car. I'll dash out the back door and meet you."

Chapter 9

After Maria left, Elizabeth continued searching Jonathan's house on her own, making her way through the maze of the mansion's dark hallways. Eventually she came to a small den at the end of a narrow hallway off the living room. A large wooden desk took up most of the floor space. Two of the walls were lined with bookcases.

Elizabeth skimmed through all the papers in the desk, none of which seemed particularly important, then moved to the bookcases. The shelves were filled mainly with classic novels. She ran her fingers over the bindings, scanning the titles. Finally she threw up her hands in surrender and exhaled loudly. "I give up."

As she turned to go, her shoulder bumped into one of the wall panels. As she rubbed the sore spot, a creaking noise sounded behind her. Elizabeth whirled around, aiming her flashlight with a shaky hand.

A recessed compartment in the wall had opened. *Jonathan's secret?* Elizabeth thought hopefully. She took a closer look and groaned. "Great! More books. Some secret I've discovered—Jonathan *reads*," she chided herself.

Elizabeth was about to turn away when she noticed one of the titles—*The Vampire Killings of Europe*. Shining her flashlight over the others, she read the titles aloud. *"Asanbosam: The Vampires of Africa. Vampire Lore of Old. In Search of Dracula . . ."* There were dozens of books, all of them about vampires and vampire legends. She pursed her lips and narrowed her eyes. *Why does Jonathan keep these hidden?* she wondered.

A cold chill ran up her spine as something clicked in the back of her mind. Without considering the wisdom of her actions, Elizabeth took several of the books and shoved them into her backpack.

On her way out, the portrait over the fireplace captured Elizabeth's attention again. She shone her flashlight on it, squinting as she studied the details. The eyes were frightening and the man did look like Jonathan, as Maria had said, but there was something else about it that nagged at

Elizabeth. She stared at the painting for a long time, trying to figure out its puzzle.

At last Elizabeth tore her gaze away from the brooding face and rushed out of the house, her shoulders stooped with the weight of Jonathan's books in her backpack.

Jessica ran through a dark, dank tunnel, trying to find her kitten. But Jasmine's meows seemed to be growing fainter. Then Jonathan appeared, his eyes beckoning to her. Jessica stretched her arms out to him in desperation, but she couldn't seem to reach him. . . .

Suddenly a small clinking sound woke her. Jessica's eyes popped open, a scream clawing at her throat. She heard the noise again and realized it was something hitting her window.

Wearing only her thin nightgown, she jumped out of bed and rushed across the room. Jonathan was standing beneath her window, silhouetted in the moonlight. Jessica took a quick breath of pure astonishment. "Am I dreaming?" she whispered. She opened the window and leaned out, bracing her elbows on the windowsill.

To her surprise, Jonathan replied. "No, you're not dreaming, Jessica—unless we both are." His eyes seemed to be pulling her toward him, as they had in her dream. "Come for a ride with me on my motorcycle," he said softly.

Jessica felt her heart leaping and flipping, as if it were performing a halftime cheerleading routine. But she hadn't forgotten the anguish Jonathan had put her through that evening. "You're a bit late, aren't you?" she snapped. "I don't know if I want to go anywhere with you."

He flashed her a wicked and utterly sexy grin. "Of course you do," he insisted.

Jessica pushed her hair behind her shoulders and raised her eyebrows. "I haven't decided to forgive you for standing me up—again."

"I'll explain everything," he promised.

Jessica swallowed, her bravado crumbling. She couldn't resist him. She backed up and quietly shut the window. Her hands trembled with excitement as she quickly got dressed.

Elizabeth kicked off her shoes and tucked her feet under her on the couch. Although it was hours past midnight, she was still in Mr. Wakefield's den, reading the books she'd taken from Jonathan's house.

She found the stuff fascinating—and horrifying. All the recent murders in Sweet Valley appeared to be bona fide vampire attacks. The descriptions of the victims—the bites on their necks, the draining of their blood—were straight off the pages of Jonathan's books.

114

Elizabeth came across a section entitled "Common Vulnerabilities of Vampires" and began reading aloud softly. "'Most vampires have to sleep in their coffins during the daylight hours. The practice is believed to have originated as a way to prevent animals from digging up the body.'"

Elizabeth shuddered. *We didn't find a coffin in Jonathan's house,* she admitted to herself. Then she remembered the antique chest in one of the upstairs bedrooms. It was large enough to hold hundreds of old sweaters or fancy linens . . . *or the body of a sleeping vampire?* she wondered.

"'Vampires cannot enter a house if they haven't been invited,'" she continued in a low voice. "'Although once invited, they may enter as often as they like.'" Elizabeth frowned, remembering when Jonathan had appeared at the door for dinner the previous Sunday. *Aren't you going to invite me inside?* he had asked her. Had he just been overly polite, she wondered, or . . .

A cold chill crept up Elizabeth's spine. She thought about his pale skin and his general strangeness. But the book also said that vampires couldn't stand the light of the sun. Jonathan went to school during the day; he had stood outside at Katrina's burial on Monday.

Elizabeth continued reading. *Vampires cast no reflection, and their image cannot be captured on film.*

"Film!" she repeated aloud, remembering the photographs Olivia had taken at Katrina's funeral. *Does Jonathan appear in any of them?* she wondered.

Just then Elizabeth heard a rapid thumping sound. She jumped, her heart in her throat. Somewhere in the house a door opened and shut.

Elizabeth tossed the book aside and crept out to the living room, holding her breath. Nothing seemed amiss. Then she heard the sound of an engine starting outside, in front of the house. Her heart skipped a beat as she rushed to the window and pulled back the curtain.

Jessica was hopping onto Jonathan's motorcycle.

Elizabeth shrieked and raced out of the house, mindless of her stocking feet. But she was too late. She could just make out the taillight of Jonathan's bike turning the corner a few blocks away.

Wait till I get my hands on you, Jessica! Elizabeth thought hotly as she burst into tears.

The glimmer of a wonderful memory played along the edges of Jessica's mind as she and Jonathan rode through the night, her arms wrapped tightly around his waist. She felt as if they were flying high above the earth, sharing a special bond that could never be broken. Deep in her gut, Jessica was totally convinced that she and Jonathan would be together forever.

They picked up speed along the Pacific Coast Highway. The wind whipped through her hair, and the salty air tickled her nose. Jessica laughed aloud, excitement tearing through her veins.

Jonathan pulled off the highway and turned onto a narrow coastal road. After several miles they arrived at a small, unmarked strip of beach. As soon as they hopped off the motorcycle, Jessica threw herself into his arms. "I've wanted to do this for days," she declared, covering his face with kisses. She giggled. "I guess I've decided to forgive you for making me wait so long."

Jonathan held her in his arms for a while, then gently pulled away. "We're almost there, Jessica."

"Where?" she asked.

He looked into her eyes. "I want to show you something."

Jessica's knees felt weak under his probing gaze. She stood aside as he moved the Harley to a spot behind a sand dune, where it couldn't be seen from the road. "Are you ready to come with me?" he asked, reaching for her hand.

"Anywhere," she whispered.

They walked hand in hand across the sandy beach, then along a path that wound through a marshy area. Finally they came to a rocky ledge that rose to a sharp cliff over the ocean. Jonathan led her to an opening in the rock. "This is it," he told her.

117

Jessica looked closer and saw that they were at the entrance of a cave. Jonathan came up behind her and put his arms around her, resting his chin on top of her head. "This is where I come when I want to find peace," he told her. "It's my special hideout. You're the only person I've brought here." He turned her around and stared into her eyes. "You're the *only* one I would ever bring to this place."

Jessica's eyes watered. She was touched beyond words. Wanting to show him how she felt, she moved her lips over his and put her whole heart into a deep, loving kiss.

By the time the kiss ended, Jessica's mind was spinning and her legs could barely support her. She looked up at Jonathan and smiled. His eyes seemed to reflect the moonlight, shining down on her like star sapphires. Jessica was dazzled by his beauty.

She didn't know what to expect when she crawled into Jonathan's cave, and she was pleasantly surprised by how cozy it was. He'd covered the floor with thick rugs, making it quite comfortable.

Jonathan gathered some driftwood and built a fire on the beach, just outside the entrance. Jessica wrapped her arms around her legs and rested her chin on her knees as she watched him work. *I'm the luckiest girl in the whole world,* she thought, awed by his graceful power.

When the fire was blazing, Jonathan crawled

into the cave beside her. Jessica rested her head on his shoulder, mesmerized by the sounds of the flames crackling and the waves crashing on the shore. "This is wonderful, Jonathan."

He gently lifted her chin and gazed into her eyes. "Finally," he whispered, "we're alone."

I don't know what to do! Elizabeth thought as she paced back and forth across the living room, frantic and terrified for her sister's safety. She considered telling her parents what had happened, but she didn't want to get Jessica in trouble. It was a long-standing tradition among the Wakefield kids—Elizabeth, Jessica, and their older brother, Steven—that they watched out for each other *without* parental involvement.

Elizabeth recalled how angry her twin had been when she'd tried to warn her about Jonathan. Jessica's fury would be a thousand times worse if she got caught because of Elizabeth. Jessica would never speak to her again.

But what if something truly horrible happens to her this time? Elizabeth asked herself. *I'd rather have an angry sister than a dead one.*

Elizabeth stopped pacing and put her hands on her hips. "How am I supposed to figure out what to do when my mind is spinning like a top?"

Taking a deep breath, she went into the kitchen

and picked up the phone. *I need the wisdom of someone who's older,* she thought as she dialed Joey's phone number.

As soon as he answered, Elizabeth began talking. "I need your advice, Joey," she said urgently. "I'm so worried about Jessica. She sneaked out of the house with Jonathan, on his motorcycle. I don't trust that guy at all," Elizabeth added.

To her surprise, Joey laughed. "That sounds like the Jessica Wakefield I knew at camp. As I recall, you worried about her then too. Face it, Elizabeth, you'll never be able to control your sister."

"You don't understand," Elizabeth protested. "I have a really bad feeling about Jonathan."

"No one ever said that you have to like your sister's boyfriends," Joey replied. "Jessica is a big girl and she can take care of herself."

Elizabeth's voice broke as she said, "She may be in terrible danger."

There was a pause on the line. "Elizabeth, you asked my advice, and this is it: Quit trying to monitor Jessica's love life and spend more time on your own. You and I haven't been alone together in ages."

"I know," Elizabeth said.

"There's a college dance on Friday. Want to go with me?" he asked.

Elizabeth sighed. "I'm still grounded, remember?"

"How could I forget?" he grumbled. "So when is your prison term over?"

"On Saturday," she replied.

"Great!" he exclaimed. "Let's spend the whole day together at the beach."

"I usually visit Enid at the hospital first thing," Elizabeth told him. "You're welcome to come along. I know you don't know her, but she was— *is*—my best friend."

"No, thanks," Joey replied. "I'm not too crazy about sick people. Call me when you get home from the hospital and we'll make our plans from there."

Elizabeth felt a surge of annoyance. "Sure," she said, anxious to end the call. "I'll see you Saturday."

What happened to the Joey I used to know at Camp Echo Mountain? she thought as she stood before the sliding glass doors and gazed at the dark backyard. Elizabeth remembered how caring and supportive he had been, especially during her battles with Nicole. *Did I fall in love with him only because Nicole wanted him too?* she wondered.

Pushing away the irritating thought, Elizabeth picked up the phone again and dialed Todd's number. When he answered, his voice was thick and groggy. "I'm sorry for waking you," Elizabeth said.

"It's OK, Elizabeth," he assured her. "What's wrong?"

Elizabeth closed her eyes, grateful for the

concern in his voice. She filled him in on Jessica's situation. "I don't know if I should keep quiet, tell my parents, or go look for her myself."

Todd cleared his throat. "I know you don't want to rat on Jessica, but this isn't just another one of her pranks. There's a serial killer out there."

"I know," Elizabeth murmured, tears streaming down her cheeks. "I'm so scared, Todd. And I don't trust Jonathan at all."

"Don't take any chances," Todd said. "Even if Jonathan isn't as bad as you think, both he and Jessica could be in danger. I think you should go wake up your parents immediately." His voice dropped to a whisper. "Call me back if you need to."

"Thanks," she returned. Feelings of tenderness for Todd welled up inside her as she hung up the phone. She remembered what a strong shoulder he had, how much she'd always counted on him. *I really miss him*, she thought wistfully.

Jessica snuggled closer to Jonathan in the cave and entwined her arms around his neck. "I love you so much," she declared.

"We have to talk," he whispered.

"So talk," she replied with a giggle, planting kisses all over his face.

"Jessica," he pleaded as he gently removed her arms from his neck.

Jessica uttered a sigh of defeat and folded her hands in her lap. "OK, talk."

Jonathan faced front, staring into the distance. The flames of the fire illuminated the finely shaped features of his beautiful face. "There was a woman once," he began.

"Is *that* what this is all about?" Jessica interrupted, hugging his arm. "I don't care about your old girlfriends, Jonathan—"

He touched his finger to her lips and smiled. "I'm very different from the other guys you know," he whispered.

"I'll say you are!" she agreed enthusiastically.

He stroked the side of her face with his thumb. "My passions are . . . different. I'm a loner. But when I first saw you, Jessica, I was stunned by your beauty. You were so—*alive*. I wanted you more than I have ever wanted any human being."

Jessica inhaled sharply, unable to help becoming excited by his words.

"But there are things you need to know about me, about my life." He gazed pensively at the fire. "I grew up in a tiny coastal village in Prussia."

Jessica frowned. "You mean *Russia?*"

"Just listen," he pleaded.

Jessica sighed and rested her head on his shoulder. She tried to concentrate on what he was saying, but her mind began to grow fuzzy.

"I came from a working family," Jonathan continued. "We weren't wealthy, but we never went hungry. My father and uncles were fishermen, as I would have been if—" He paused and took a deep, shaky breath. "I remember looking out over the Baltic Sea, trying to feel satisfied with my life. But I wanted more. I'd see members of the aristocracy, with their fine clothes and gold watches, and my heart would burn with envy."

Jessica drifted into a dreamy state, his words flowing over her like warm honey. For some reason, a vague memory of staring into the dark eyes of a raven teased her. A crazy thought edged its way into Jessica's brain, just out of her reach. . . .

Suddenly Jonathan jumped up and scrambled out of the cave. Jessica frowned, confused, as she watched him toss sand over their fire to put out the flames.

A moment later she heard what had startled him. Loud voices were coming from a short distance down the beach. Her mind snapped to attention, pushing away the soothing fog. A shiver of fear raced up and down her spine. "Oh, my gosh, what if it's the murderer?" she cried softly.

Jonathan crawled back into the cave and pulled her close. "I guarantee you," he whispered in her ear, "it's not the killer."

Chapter 10

Elizabeth knocked softly on her parents' door, hoping that she was doing the right thing—and that it wasn't too late. A moment later her mother opened the door and stepped out into the hall, yawning as she tied the belt of her green terry-cloth robe. "What's the matter, Liz?" she whispered, her blue-green eyes filled with concern.

"I'm sorry to wake you, Mom. It's Jessica," Elizabeth replied.

Alice Wakefield patted her mouth as she yawned again. "Is she sick?"

"No, she's gone. She sneaked out with Jonathan, on his motorcycle."

Her mother's eyes widened in a look of alarm. "Do you know where they've gone?"

Elizabeth shook her head, suddenly feeling

very young and frightened. "I'm worried about her. And I don't like Jonathan," she admitted. "I think he's—" She checked herself before she blurted out her vampire suspicions. "—bad news."

"I agree with you there." Her mother rubbed her hand over her eyes and groaned. "I don't believe this. He seemed like such a charming guy when he came over for dinner. I was certainly fooled." She ducked her head into her bedroom and woke her husband, then turned back to Elizabeth. "You're sure you have no idea where they might be?" she asked.

Elizabeth shook her head. *Where would a vampire take a girl on a date?* she wondered wryly.

Her mother grabbed the phone extension in the hall and punched in the number to the Sweet Valley Police Department. "Wait till I get my hands on your sister! Jessica is going to be grounded until she's forty."

Ned Wakefield stepped into the hall, grumbling and scratching the back of his head. "Who are you calling at this hour?" he asked his wife.

"The police," she answered. "Jessica skipped out—" She stopped in midsentence as someone apparently picked up at the other end of the line. "Hello, I'd like to report an emergency, please," she said.

Elizabeth told her father the rest of the story.

He cursed under his breath, shaking his head.

Alice Wakefield placed her hand over the mouthpiece. "How long ago did they leave?" she asked Elizabeth.

"I'm not sure," Elizabeth replied. "Maybe a half hour."

Her mother relayed the information to the police and gave them a physical description of Jessica. "That's right, Officer. We believe she's with Jonathan Cain and that they're riding a Harley-Davidson motorcycle, black with silver trim. I know it doesn't sound like an emergency, but she's breaking curfew, and with the serial killer on the loose . . ."

She hung up and turned to Elizabeth and Mr. Wakefield. "All we can do now is wait," she said.

Elizabeth choked back a sob. "I'm so sorry I didn't come and wake you as soon as Jessica left. I wasted so much time trying to figure out what to do."

Her father put his arms around Elizabeth's and her mother's shoulders. "Jessica should've known better. This is entirely her responsibility," he said.

"I know, but if anything happens to her, I'll never forgive myself," Elizabeth cried.

The sounds grew louder. Someone was definitely heading toward the cave. Jessica held her breath, her arms wrapped tightly around Jonathan.

Her blood felt like ice. Despite Jonathan's assurances, she was afraid they were about to meet Sweet Valley's serial killer.

Suddenly the bright beam of a flashlight stabbed into her eyes, blinding her. Jessica screamed, sure she was going to be murdered.

A gruff voice shouted, "Sweet Valley Police. Come out slowly with your hands up!"

Jessica exhaled with a shriek. She was incredibly relieved—but only for a second. A new worry replaced her fear of being killed. *I'm in big trouble now!* she thought. She scooted out of the cave with Jonathan, both of them holding their hands high in the air. Four police officers were crouched around the opening of the cave, each aiming a gun right at her and Jonathan.

"Don't shoot us!" Jessica pleaded.

"Just keep your hands up where we can see them," one of the officers commanded.

"We didn't mean any harm, really. We just lost track of time. Is it really after ten o'clock?" Jessica babbled nervously.

Jonathan remained quiet, his expression solemn and respectful. But Jessica noticed a glint of amusement in his gorgeous blue eyes.

The officers finally lowered their weapons. One of them asked for identification while another stepped back and mumbled into his radio,

"Unit seventy-three . . . just a couple of kids . . ."

Jonathan handed over his entire wallet. Jessica realized she hadn't brought anything with her when she'd sneaked out of the house. She dug through her pockets, hoping to find something with her name on it. "I wasn't driving tonight, so I didn't bring my license," she explained.

She finally found a crumpled library pass that she'd wheedled out of one of her teachers weeks earlier but never used. "Will this do?" she asked as she held it out to one of the officers.

He took it and examined it for a moment by the light of his flashlight. "I don't think you two understand the seriousness of this situation," he said, handing the pass back to Jessica. "The town curfew was established for your protection, but it's not optional. Breaking the curfew is against the law."

"We didn't mean to," Jessica interjected, putting on her best innocent expression.

The officer glared at her, his nostrils flaring. "We're not playing games here, young lady!" he barked. "You're lucky we came along. This area is extremely dangerous. We've found blood samples matching two of the three victims in this immediate location—strong evidence that the killer came here after committing those murders."

Jessica gasped in terror. She and Jonathan had wandered right into the killer's lair. *We really could have been murdered!* she realized, trembling. *And Jonathan—* Jessica clutched his hand tightly. *He's been coming to this place by himself!* She was thankful that nothing horrible had happened to him.

A nagging thought seeped into her mind. When the police had approached the cave, Jonathan had said he *guaranteed* it wasn't the killer. *How could he have been so sure?* she wondered. Elizabeth's hysterical accusation popped into Jessica's head. *She couldn't possibly be right, could she? Jonathan— involved with the murders?* Jessica asked herself.

Jonathan turned to her and smiled, giving her a conspiratorial wink. Jessica sighed, and her doubts instantly vanished.

The police officers continued to scold them for several minutes, as if Jessica and Jonathan were naughty children. Then the officers questioned them about anything suspicious they might have noticed in the area.

Jessica jumped as a burst of static came over the police radio. She groaned to herself as she listened to the broadcast message.

"Sixteen-year-old girl reported missing from her home . . . Jessica Wakefield, Caucasian, blond hair, blue eyes . . . believed to be in the company of one Jonathan Cain, also Caucasian . . ."

She clamped her hand over her mouth. Until that moment, she had hoped to sneak back into her house without her parents finding out that she'd ever left. "I think I'm in terrible trouble," she murmured to Jonathan.

A strange look glittered in his eyes. "It won't be for long," he murmured, squeezing her hand.

Elizabeth and her parents ran outside as the police cruiser pulled up in front of the house. When Jessica climbed out of the car, obviously unharmed, her mother burst into tears and hugged her tightly.

"We found her and her boyfriend at the beach." The police officer described the location of a cave a few miles south of the town beach. "It's just about the most dangerous spot they could've picked for a date," he said, shaking his head. "We've found evidence linking it to the recent murders in Sweet Valley and have been patrolling that area for days."

Elizabeth saw her father's face pale. "Thank you for bringing our daughter home safely," he said. "I assure you this will never happen again."

"See that it doesn't," the officer warned. "The curfew is still in effect, and we expect better cooperation in the future."

As the police drove away Jessica was marched into the house, flanked by a parent on either side, with Elizabeth following behind them. Mr. Wakefield

131

slammed the door shut and glared at Jessica, his eyes flashing with anger. "This little stunt of yours, young lady—" He inhaled sharply, visibly shaken. "And that Jonathan," he raged. "I can't believe he had the nerve to come here and take you out in the middle of the night—on a motorcycle!"

Jessica opened her mouth, as if to speak, but her father cut her off. "Go right to bed!" he ordered.

Jessica nodded meekly. Before she left, she turned to Elizabeth.

Assuming her twin had figured out who had gotten her in trouble, Elizabeth braced herself for a piercing glare of fiery wrath. Instead, she saw a dreamy, faraway expression in Jessica's eyes. *She looks like she's in a trance,* Elizabeth realized, shocked.

A knife of cold fear twisted in her gut. She knew that the night's terror was only the beginning. *And Jessica is heading straight into a nightmare,* she thought.

Jessica hit the snooze button on her radio alarm another time and snuggled under the covers, as she usually did on school days. Suddenly she felt a hand on her shoulder, shaking her. "Go 'way," she whined.

The shaking continued. "Come on, Jess," Elizabeth commanded in a bossy-big-sister voice. "You have to get up. It's late."

Jessica hugged her pillow tighter. "Five more minutes." The image of Jonathan's face floated into her mind. She smiled, remembering their romantic escapade. Already she longed to be with him again.

"Mom and Dad want to talk to you," Elizabeth said.

Something in her tone struck a nerve. Jessica opened her eyes and sat up, pushing her hair out of her face. She caught sight of Elizabeth standing over her, scowling.

Jessica glared at her. "I'm still mad at you for the terrible things you said about Jonathan."

"So go ahead and be mad," Elizabeth responded tersely. "But you still have to get out of that bed—*now*."

Jessica made a face at her sister's retreating back. *She should run away and join the circus as a lion tamer,* Jessica thought snidely. *It would be Elizabeth's ideal job—getting paid for cracking a whip every day.*

Jessica plodded to the bathroom the twins shared and stared at herself in the mirror. She was surprised at how good she looked that morning, even though she hadn't gotten much sleep. Her eyes were radiant, her skin flushed and glowing. "Being in love does wonders for a girl's complexion," she said with a giggle.

Despite's Elizabeth dire warning about being

late, Jessica took her time getting dressed. She changed her clothes several times, trying to choose the perfect outfit to wear to school. She finally settled on a slinky blue skirt and a red silk tank top with her new silver chain belt. Striking a pose in front of her full-length mirror, Jessica admired her reflection. *Sexy and sophisticated,* she thought. *Jonathan, watch out!*

By the time she'd gathered her things and headed downstairs, Jessica's spirits were soaring. Humming to herself, she breezed into the kitchen. Her parents and sister were sitting at the table with grave expressions on their faces. "Good morning, everyone," Jessica said cheerfully.

No one returned the greeting.

Elizabeth rose to her feet and picked up her backpack. "I'd better go," she murmured.

Jessica reached over and grabbed a slice of toast from the table. "I'm ready too."

"Not yet, Jessica," her father responded. "Sit down. We have a few things to discuss."

Jessica's back stiffened. "What's going on?"

Her mother turned to Elizabeth. "Go ahead and take the Jeep. Your father or I will give Jessica a ride to school this morning."

Jessica watched her sister leave, then faced her parents. "I have history first period and I can't be late," she announced nervously.

134

"This won't take long," her father said with an edge to his voice.

Jessica sat down and clutched her hands together in her lap. "I'm sorry about last night," she began, trying to sound sincere. "I promise I'll never do something like that again."

"I'll say you won't!" her father bellowed. "Your recklessness amazes me, Jessica. There's a serial killer on the loose! And you know how we feel about motorcycles. Have you forgotten that your cousin Rexy was killed in a motorcycle crash? And that Elizabeth nearly died in one too? You've broken our rules, the police department's curfew—"

"I know, but it won't happen again. Believe me," Jessica pleaded.

Her father exhaled sharply. "Considering your recent actions, the only thing I believe right now is that you have absolutely no common sense. Your behavior was totally unacceptable," he declared. "From now on, you're grounded indefinitely."

Jessica's jaw dropped. She turned a pleading look to her mother. But instead of softening, Alice Wakefield's expression grew harder. "I never want to go through a scare like last night's again," she said, her voice trembling.

"Jonathan Cain is strictly off-limits," Ned Wakefield added swiftly.

Jessica gasped. "For how long?"

135

"Permanently," her father responded. "He's proven himself to be completely untrustworthy."

"You can't blame him," Jessica protested. "He didn't force me to go with him. How do you know it wasn't my idea in the first place?"

Her father glowered at her. "I don't care whose idea it was. At best, Jonathan Cain is a bad influence. And you are forbidden to see him ever again."

Jessica's eyes filled with hot tears. She couldn't believe her parents were trying to take away the most important thing in her life—her relationship with Jonathan. She wanted to scream at them, but she knew they would never understand. *No one can understand how deeply I love Jonathan,* she thought.

"Now get ready for school," her mother ordered. "I'll drive you on my way to my first meeting."

"School?" Jessica screeched. "I'm not going to school—not today or ever. If I can't see Jonathan, I don't want to see anyone at all." It pleased her to see the shock on her parents' faces.

Jessica stormed out of the kitchen and ran upstairs to her room, sobbing. She slammed the door soundly, then leaned back against it as she sank to the floor. *They can't keep me away from Jonathan,* she silently raged.

She and Jonathan were bound to each other by a deep, solid love and a desperate need. No one could see into her soul as he could or make her heart soar like a bird through the heavens. *He is my destiny, and I* will *be with him,* she vowed. *No matter what the price.*

As soon as Elizabeth arrived at school, she rushed straight to the *Oracle* office, weaving her way through the morning crowd in the halls. The idea of Jonathan as a vampire had taken hold in her mind, and Elizabeth was determined to check it out, as crazy as it seemed.

She searched through the file of material for the *Oracle* issue devoted to Katrina, but the photographs weren't there. A few minutes later, when Olivia walked in, Elizabeth immediately pounced on her. "Where are the photos you took at the funeral?" she asked urgently.

Olivia raised her eyebrows. "And good morning to you, Elizabeth. As a matter of fact, I have them right here." She pulled a thick manila envelope from her backpack. "You're welcome to see them, as soon as you tell me what's going on."

Elizabeth hesitated for a moment. "I want to see if there's a photograph of Jonathan Cain in the set," she admitted.

Olivia chuckled as she handed over the envelope. "I'm sure I snapped a few nice shots of him. But I had no idea you were one of his followers.

Does this mean you're going to dye your hair and wear black lipstick?" she teased.

Elizabeth flashed her a crooked smile and carried them over to an empty table. "I'm just looking for a picture of him," she said, spreading out the photos. "I'm not planing to join his fan club."

"That's good," Olivia remarked. "I don't think black hair would go with your skin tone or your personality."

"I'll take that as a compliment," Elizabeth muttered as she studied the photos. "You're sure you got Jonathan in some of these?"

Olivia joined her at the table. "Let's see. . . ." She placed a photo in front of Elizabeth. "Here, take this one. It's not of Jonathan, but I thought you might like to keep it."

Elizabeth looked at the photograph and smiled wistfully. She and Todd were standing side by side, holding hands. "Thanks," she said softly.

"But where's Jonathan?" Olivia asked, frowning. She passed Elizabeth a photograph of Amy, her cousin Mimi, Jessica, and Lila. "I'd like to enlarge this one to a full page," Olivia commented.

Elizabeth gazed at the sad faces in the picture and nodded. "It certainly captures the mood of the day." She set it aside and continued looking through the rest of the photos. "Jonathan doesn't seem to be in any of these," she said.

Olivia's eyes narrowed. "I could have sworn I took some of him." She flipped through the pile again. "Here," she said hopefully, pointing to a group shot of several guys. "No, wait—that's not him." She looked up and shrugged. "I'm really sorry, Liz. Do you need it right away?"

Elizabeth shook her head as she studied a photograph of Bruce, Kirk, and Tim taken during the service. She was sure that Jonathan had been standing right behind them during the funeral. She remembered seeing him when she'd turned around to greet Maria.

So why can't I see him in this photograph? Elizabeth wondered.

Chapter 11

"Hold it right there, Elizabeth," Maria said, raising her hand. "You've just passed my limit of believability. Maybe Jessica was right—you *are* beginning to sound completely nuts."

Elizabeth exhaled wearily. She and Maria were alone in the *Oracle* office, discussing Elizabeth's research on vampire legends and her suspicions about the recent murders. "It sounds unbelievable to me too," she conceded. "But think about it, Maria. The victims were left with a strange bite mark, and their blood was drained."

"And you think a vampire guzzled it down?" Maria replied, glaring at her incredulously.

Elizabeth nodded and braced herself for Maria's reaction to the rest of her theory. "I think the vampire is Jonathan Cain."

Maria let out a hoot of laughter. "Poor Liz. Maybe I should walk you down to the nurse's office."

Elizabeth ignored the sarcasm and took out the photograph of Bruce, Kirk, and Tim that Olivia had taken at the funeral. "How do you explain this?" she demanded, waving it under Maria's nose.

Maria grabbed it from Elizabeth's hand. "What is it?" she asked, studying the photograph.

"Proof," Elizabeth declared.

Maria frowned. "How is this proof?"

"Jonathan was standing directly behind those guys, but he's not in the photo, is he? And he doesn't appear in any of them," Elizabeth added. "Don't you think that's strange?"

Maria shrugged. "Maybe he moved at the very instant the picture was shot. And aren't vampires supposed to avoid the sunlight? Jonathan comes to school and rides a motorcycle during the day."

"According to what I've read, not all vampires are alike," Elizabeth informed her. "They're as different from each other as people are. Maybe some vampires can withstand the rays of the sun. After all, it wasn't too long ago that everyone believed it was impossible for a human being to run faster than a four-minute mile."

"And you think Jonathan is the record-breaking athlete of the Vampire Olympics?" Maria laughed at her own joke. "Jonathan Cain, winner of the gold medal in the sunbathing competition," she added dramatically.

"Just postpone your judgment for a while longer," Elizabeth pleaded. "I need your help. Maybe I *have* gone completely nuts. But what if I'm right?"

Maria's eyes narrowed. "You're really serious about this, aren't you?"

"Yes," Elizabeth replied. "*Dead* serious."

Maria pursed her lips and stared at Elizabeth for a long moment. "OK, but let's just get one thing straight," Maria said sharply. "I'm helping you only because you're my friend. I don't believe any of this vampire baloney."

Elizabeth breathed a sigh of relief. "Thanks."

"So where do we start?" Maria asked.

Elizabeth sat down in front of one of the *Oracle's* computers. "Right here," she said. She knew from past experience that computers were very useful when it came to confirming suspicions about a person.

Using her *Oracle* code, Elizabeth logged onto a research network and typed in the word *vampire*. She was surprised when the computer indicated almost a thousand listings on the topic.

Maria pulled up a chair next to her. "I never knew this stuff was so popular. Try limiting the search to vampires in California," she suggested.

"I don't know what that would tell us," Elizabeth countered. "But I guess it's worth a try."

They flipped through the titles of several articles that had appeared in major newspapers over the years. "Hey, look at that one," Maria said. "'Mount Creshnor Under Siege—Seventh Murder Blamed on Vampire Cult.' That's in northern California, isn't it?"

"I think it's near the Oregon border." Elizabeth hit the keyboard command to print the article.

Maria rushed over to the printer and grabbed the first page. "OK, what have we got?" She began reading aloud. "'Mount Creshnor police chief Roger Marks reports the slain body of Tom Brown was found last night . . . drained of blood, with a suspicious incision on his neck.'" She fell silent as her eyes skimmed the page. "Get this, Elizabeth. The victim was a 'seventeen-year-old colored youth.'" Maria looked up and wrinkled her nose. "We haven't been *colored* for decades. When was this article published?"

"1938," Elizabeth replied, her mind whirling. "I wonder if . . ." She switched over to the newspaper's index for that year and began scrolling down the alphabetical list.

Maria came up behind her. "What are you looking for now?"

"Nothing, it seems." Elizabeth sighed and

rubbed her eyes. "I was checking to see if the name *Cain* was published in the Mount Creshnor newspaper."

"What about that one, all the way on the bottom?" Maria asked. "John Cayne. It's close."

"You're right." Elizabeth clicked the cursor on the name. An image began to form on the screen, gradually revealing a grainy photograph with a caption that read, "'Mount Creshnor High School Graduating Class of 1938.'"

"Elizabeth, look at the caption!" Maria said, her eyes wide. "The very last line."

"'Missing from photo, John Cayne,'" Elizabeth read. "Just like Jonathan Cain." An icy shiver ran up her spine. She knew she was on the right track.

She scrolled down to the section that listed each student's extracurricular activities, club affiliations, and honors received. "Look at this, Maria. There's only one item listed for John Cayne— 'Voted most popular boy in the senior class.'"

Maria sat back, her arms folded tightly. "That does seem strange. If he didn't join any school clubs, play sports, or hold an office in student government, how did he get so popular?"

Elizabeth grunted. "It sounds exactly like Jonathan. He struts around with that big mystery act of his, without ever doing anything worthwhile, and everyone falls all over him as if he were the greatest celebrity in the world. It's sickening."

"But this is all so crazy!" Maria countered.

Elizabeth tapped her fingers on the edge of the desk. "Look at the evidence, Maria. The police found traces of blood that match Dean Maddingly's and Jean Hartley's in the area of the cave where Jonathan took Jessica Monday night. We also have the fact that Enid said Jonathan's name when she woke up last Saturday. And we found the vampire books in his house."

"*You* found them," Maria corrected her. "I still can't believe you had the nerve to steal them. But this is still so far-fetched. Jonathan Cain, a *vampire?*"

"Everything adds up," Elizabeth insisted. "I read that vampires have the ability to draw people to themselves and to control their minds by mesmerizing them. That could be how John Cayne became the most popular guy in Mount Creshnor's class of 1938 and why everyone is crazy about Jonathan Cain.

"It would also explain the glassy-eyed zombie that's masquerading as my twin sister," Elizabeth continued, a note of bitterness in her voice. "I don't think she even cares who ratted on her when she sneaked out with Jonathan. The old Jessica would have been out for revenge."

"So what does this all mean?" Maria asked. "Do you think John Cayne is related to Jonathan Cain?"

"I don't know," Elizabeth replied. "But I'm more convinced than ever that Jonathan is not a normal person and that if we don't stop him, more will die."

How did everything fall apart? Todd asked himself as he tossed his athletic bag into the backseat of his BMW after basketball practice. For days he'd gone around feeling completely numb, as if he were surrounded by his own personal gray cloud. The whole world had turned crazy. Three people were dead, *murdered;* Enid Rollins was in a coma; and Elizabeth was going out with Joey Mason.

Instead of heading straight home, Todd drove around aimlessly, wondering if his life would ever get back to normal. *Not without Elizabeth,* he thought.

Todd found himself heading toward the hospital and realized that he was anxious to see Enid. Worrying about her had been a constant weight on his mind since he'd learned of the attack.

A short time later Todd hovered in the doorway of Enid's hospital room. Her mother was sitting in a chair next to the bed. She looked up from her book and smiled warmly. "Come in, Todd. It's so nice to see you."

"How is she?" he asked. He stepped inside and stood awkwardly at the foot of Enid's bed.

Ms. Rollins's eyes filled with tears.

"I'm sorry," Todd mumbled nervously. Obviously it hadn't been the right question to ask. He turned his gaze to Enid and felt even worse. Her face and neck were covered with bruises in various shades of purple. One of her eyelids was swollen. Tubes were stuck in her mouth and up her nose. She looked nothing like the Enid he knew.

Ms. Rollins swallowed hard. "Have a seat," she invited. "Actually, we're very hopeful. Enid woke up for an instant a few days ago. The doctors say that's a good sign."

Todd nodded and sat in one of the bright orange chairs. A nurse came in a few minutes later and suggested that Ms. Rollins take a break. "This young man seems capable of watching over your daughter for a few minutes," she said, nodding at Todd.

"I'll stay right here until you come back," he assured Enid's mother.

When he was alone, Todd turned his attention back to the girl in the bed. *The patient—formerly known as Enid Rollins,* he thought, shuddering. The horror suddenly became real. *She may not make it,* he realized.

Todd wondered how Elizabeth was holding up under the strain. He'd watched her during lunch at school that day. She had seemed so distraught. The frightened, vulnerable look in her eyes had tugged at his heart.

Suddenly, soft footsteps sounded behind him. He turned around and saw Elizabeth standing there in the hospital room's doorway—as if she'd stepped out of his imagination. Todd's pulse quickened at the sight of her. Neither spoke; they stood, staring at each other, for a long moment.

Elizabeth ran the tip of her tongue over her top lip, drawing his attention to her mouth. Todd groaned to himself. He wanted so badly to kiss her, his hands were shaking.

"I'm glad you're here, Todd," Elizabeth said. "I want to thank you for your help Monday night. I was so worried about Jessica, and I couldn't think straight."

Todd shrugged. "Call me anytime. I'll always care about you, Liz." *And love you,* he added silently.

Elizabeth smiled, then walked over to the side of the bed and took Enid's limp hand in hers. "I keep thinking there was something I could have done to prevent this from happening," she whispered, tears spilling down her cheeks.

Todd felt a lump in his throat as he watched Elizabeth. A million thoughts whirled around in his head, but he couldn't think of any words to say to her. He was also filled with regrets, about a lot of things.

"I want her to wake up and tell us who did this to her," Elizabeth said, her voice trembling with emotion.

"There's a meeting at Bruce's house on Saturday," he told her. "If the police haven't made an arrest by then, everyone is getting together to figure out a way to catch the killer on our own."

Elizabeth's jaw tightened as she looked up at him. "I don't know, Todd. Somehow the sound of that makes me nervous."

"The police aren't doing enough," Todd declared emphatically. "It's been almost two weeks since Katrina was killed, and they still don't have a single suspect in custody."

"I know," Elizabeth agreed. "But a mob scene at Bruce's house doesn't seem like a good idea. Bruce Patman isn't the most reasonable guy when things get heated."

"Then maybe you should come," Todd said. He had his own reasons for wanting Elizabeth there. *I want to see her as often as I can, even if she's with another guy,* he reasoned.

Elizabeth gripped the side rail of Enid's hospital bed. "Maybe I will," she replied. "But I'm going to try something else first."

Todd wondered what she was planning to do. It was on the tip of his tongue to ask her, but he decided to let it go. *She's not my girlfriend,* he realized sadly. *I don't have the right to know what's going on in Elizabeth's life anymore.*

✿ ✿ ✿

Friday afternoon, Jessica waited for Jonathan outside Ms. Dalton's classroom before the start of their French class. After thinking long and hard about their relationship for the past few days, Jessica had finally decided to take a big step. She only hoped Jonathan would agree with her plans.

Her heart leaped when she spotted him coming toward her. *He's so beautiful,* she thought. It seemed every time Jessica saw him, she loved him more and more.

Jonathan pulled her into the doorway of an empty classroom and leaned over her, brushing his lips across her forehead. She wrapped her arms around his back and held him close. "I can't stand being apart from you," she whispered urgently. "Let's get out of here—*now.*"

He wove his fingers through her hair, caressing the back of her neck. Jessica could feel his hand trembling.

"What about French class?" he asked. "Do you want to miss the review for Monday's vocabulary exam?"

"How can you possibly think I'd rather sit through a boring French review?" Jessica noticed a glimmer of laughter in his eyes and shoved him playfully. "This isn't the time to tease, Jonathan."

He tucked a strand of her hair behind her ear. "I don't deserve a girl like you," he whispered solemnly.

Jessica tried to smile, but a sob broke through her bravado. "I can't stand it anymore, Jonathan. I've missed you so much, I feel like my heart is dying. I'd hoped that my parents would lighten up after a few days, but I'm still grounded for life. And I'm still forbidden to see you."

"I don't blame your family for trying to protect you from me," he replied gravely. "I only wish I could do the same." He pulled her into a tight embrace.

Just then the bell rang, signaling the start of last period. Jessica looked up into Jonathan's eyes. "It would be terribly rude to walk in late."

Jonathan smiled tenderly and entwined his fingers with hers. "OK, Jessica," he said. "Let's get out of here. I seem to remember that we never got a chance to finish our talk Monday night."

"Are you sure about this?" Maria asked as Elizabeth parked the Jeep outside the Sweet Valley police station. "Maybe we should wait until we have something more concrete."

Elizabeth turned off the engine and pocketed the keys. "We don't have time," she replied. "Bruce has the whole school stirred up. If we don't present our evidence to the police right away, someone may get hurt. Believe me, with Bruce in charge Saturday night, the scene at the Patman mansion may turn very ugly."

Maria pulled down the vanity mirror and finger-combed her short hair into place. "I'm so nervous about this. And I can't believe you lied to Mr. Collins!"

Elizabeth winced. She'd told Mr. Collins, her favorite teacher and the faculty advisor for the *Oracle*, that she and Maria needed to interview the police for an article about the town curfew. He'd automatically written out a special pass allowing them to leave school early, and he'd commended Elizabeth for having come up with "another great idea."

"Maybe I *will* write that article," Elizabeth murmured. *Then what I told him won't be a lie,* she reasoned.

"Just promise me one thing, Liz." Maria turned with a serious, direct look in her brown eyes. "Promise me you won't mention the vampire thing. It'll just make us look crazy."

Elizabeth raised her right hand. "I promise."

Jessica was surprised when Jonathan brought her to the same beach as he had Monday night. "Are you sure this is wise, considering that the killer comes here?" she asked as they hopped off the bike.

"Trust me," he replied, reaching for her hand.

"Always." She smiled and hurried to his side.

They walked hand in hand along the beach,

toward the cave. The sun was shining brightly. A flock of seagulls circled overhead and swerved out toward the horizon. The ocean was at high tide, the waves crashing with full force on the shore. Jessica's heart overflowed with sheer joy.

The swelling tide had created a wide, rushing stream across the path to the cave. Jessica was surprised when Jonathan stopped abruptly and turned to her with a pained expression on his face.

"What's wrong?" she asked.

"Maybe this wasn't such a good idea," he said, gazing at the swirling stream.

Jessica nodded. "I don't want to take the chance of meeting up with a serial killer on this path," she remarked.

An unreadable expression passed across Jonathan's face. "Yes, of course. The serial killer." He suggested they sit in the shade of an abandoned shack a few yards away.

Jessica frowned. "It's such a nice day. Wouldn't you rather sit in the sun?"

Jonathan ran his fingertip over the surface of his ring. "No, I wouldn't."

Something flickered in the back of Jessica's mind—a thought, a nagging doubt. She pushed it aside firmly and flashed him a bright smile. "You're absolutely right, Jonathan. Sunlight is terrible for the skin. Causes wrinkles too."

They snuggled together in the cool shade, resting their backs against the side of the shack. Jessica closed her eyes and sighed. It felt so wonderful to be with Jonathan again, at last.

She felt the gentle touch of his lips brushing against hers. Jessica smiled and opened her eyes. He was looking at her with a hot gaze that seemed to reach into the very core of her heart. "We belong together," she whispered.

A sad expression fluttered across his face. "My life has taught me a painful lesson. We can't always have everything our hearts cry out for."

Jessica raised her chin defiantly. "The only reason we can't be together is because other people keep getting in our way," she countered. "That's why I've decided to leave home." She glanced at Jonathan, unsure of his reaction. *What if he doesn't want me as much I want him?* she feared.

But the tender look in his eyes assured her he did. Jonathan lowered his lips to hers for a glorious kiss that went on and on, until her whole body was trembling.

"Oh, Jessica," he groaned, tearing his lips away from hers. "I wish I had the strength to resist you."

"I don't want you to," she replied boldly, wrapping her arms around his neck.

"You don't know what you're getting into," he whispered. "My life isn't one you would want to lead."

Jessica shook her head, meeting his gaze. "There's nothing you or anyone can say to change my mind. I'm yours, completely," she proclaimed, realizing how true it was. She couldn't imagine any life without Jonathan.

"But Jessica—" he began, his voice filled with anguish.

She scooted around so that she was kneeling in the soft sand directly in front of him. "I love you," she declared. "Since the moment I first saw you, you have been my destiny. I'll follow you anywhere."

Jonathan pulled her into his arms and moaned her name. He pressed his lips roughly against hers. Jessica sensed his desperation and responded with her own fierce longing.

As the kiss continued, Jessica felt dazed and weak, her mind whirling out of control. Jonathan's lips left hers, dropping kisses across her face and down the length of her throat, sucking gently at the side of her neck.

Suddenly a cold, prickling sensation skittered along Jessica's spine. Then Jonathan looked deeply into her eyes and the feeling disappeared. A peaceful warmth came over her, soothing her. Jessica sighed, a happy smile on her lips.

"Yes, my darling," Jonathan whispered. "You and I shall be together."

Chapter 12

"I'm positive Jonathan Cain had something to do with the murders," Elizabeth insisted.

Seated across a scarred wooden table from her and Maria, Detective Cabrini of the SVPD Homicide Division nodded politely. "Thanks for stopping by, girls." He rose to his feet, his expression bland. "We always appreciate the input of concerned citizens like yourselves."

Elizabeth's jaw dropped. She and Maria had been kept waiting in the lobby for nearly an hour, and now, after a two-minute meeting, they were being dismissed. Something inside her snapped. "You don't believe a word of this, do you?" she accused him.

Maria touched her arm. "Come on, Liz, let's go," she urged. "We said what we came to say."

"But Enid Rollins came out of her coma and actually said his name," Elizabeth reminded the detective, ignoring Maria.

Detective Cabrini sat back down and leaned forward, bracing his elbows on the beaten-up table. "This case is freaking out the whole town." He looked at Elizabeth directly, his gray eyes filled with weary anger. "I know your father well and I have great respect for your family, so don't take this personally. But if I had a dollar for every crackpot who's been turning in 'evidence' . . ." He made a laughing sound at the back of his throat. "Let's just say I could retire in high style. Since the wire services picked up the story, I've been getting calls from as far away as New Zealand."

Maria turned to Elizabeth with a pleading look in her brown eyes. "Let's go," she whispered. Again Elizabeth ignored her.

"At last count," Detective Cabrini continued, "sixty-eight people have turned in their mothers-in-law, and I've got a Japanese psychic on the line right now waiting to tell me about her dream last night. She's been calling every day around this time."

"But Katrina was killed right in Jonathan's house," Elizabeth insisted.

"Jonathan Cain was considered and dismissed as a suspect the night of his party," the detective replied. "All the evidence against him is circumstantial. And as for Enid Rollins—there's no proof that she was naming her attacker when she whispered his name. She may have been calling for him," he added. "We spoke to Jonathan's father by telephone. Everything seems to check out."

"Are you sure it was Jonathan's father?" Elizabeth asked.

The detective raised his eyebrows. "Not that I owe you any explanations, Ms. Wakefield, but yes, we did check out the call. It was made from a hotel in Germany."

"But that doesn't prove—" Elizabeth stopped and took a deep, shaky breath. *Sorry, Maria,* she thought, knowing she was about to break her promise. "There's more, Detective Cabrini," Elizabeth began.

Maria gasped and pinched her under the table.

Elizabeth clenched her jaw. "We have reason to believe that Jonathan is a vampire."

At that the detective whistled incredulously and clapped his hands together. "Would you like to speak to that Japanese psychic on the phone?" he offered, laughing.

Elizabeth's mouth tightened. She wasn't amused.

"That went well," Maria muttered sarcastically as she and Elizabeth left the police station a few minutes later. "The detective didn't believe a single word we said."

Elizabeth felt ready to explode with frustration. "I thought the idea of everyone coming up with a plan at Bruce's house tomorrow night was crazy. But maybe the kids *should* take matters into their own hands."

Saturday evening, Jessica lay across her unmade bed, wondering how she was going to slip by her prison-guard sister. Their parents had gone out for the evening, which left Elizabeth as the only barrier keeping Jessica from Jonathan. But getting around her wasn't going to be easy. Jessica had managed to outsmart her twin in the past, but lately Elizabeth had become more astute.

Jessica rolled over onto her back and stared at the ceiling. *Why can't anyone understand how I feel?* she thought. Her longing for Jonathan felt like a physical ache. But her family had been watching over her every minute for days, as if she were a dangerous criminal. Didn't they understand that they were forcing her to choose between them and Jonathan?

Tears filled Jessica's eyes, spilling down the sides of her face. *Since when is falling deeply in love a crime?* she asked herself.

Jessica heard a car pulling into the driveway. Curious, she jumped off her bed and ran to the window just in time to see her twin getting into

Maria Slater's Mercedes. "Why, that little slacker!" Jessica muttered with a giggle. "So much for Officer Lizzy, my dedicated watchdog."

Cheering her good luck, Jessica sprang into action.

The instant Elizabeth got into the car, Maria shoved a bunch of papers at her. "I'm sorry I ever doubted you," Maria announced.

Elizabeth buckled her seat belt and looked at the pages on her lap. "What is all this?" she asked.

"I had a busy day in cyberspace," Maria remarked.

Elizabeth frowned. "What are you talking about?"

Maria shot her a quick sideways glance. "Vampires. I looked up more information on the Internet."

Elizabeth began skimming through the material in the dim light inside the car. At a stop sign, Maria reached over and popped open the glove compartment. "I think there's a flashlight in there somewhere."

Elizabeth found it and turned it on, then continued to read.

"Check out the section on symbols and talismans—the part I've marked," Maria suggested.

"Let's see. . . ." Elizabeth flipped through the pages until she found the highlighted passages. "Here it is. 'Tools of the vampire . . . a talisman such as a pendant or ring may enable a vampire to

161

overcome a particular vulnerability to some extent, while increasing all others . . . for instance, in lessening the deadly effects of the sun's rays, the talisman may actually increase susceptibility to destruction by fire.'"

"And have you noticed the ring Jonathan always wears?" Maria asked.

Elizabeth nodded, picturing his ornate wooden band inlaid with silver and onyx. A vague thought fluttered through her mind.

"Up until I read that section," Maria continued, "I kept thinking that everything we found could be explained by coincidence. The one point that kept bothering me was that Jonathan went outside during the day. That ring might be his talisman."

Elizabeth gasped. "Oh, my gosh, that's it!" she exclaimed. "The *ring!* It's in the portrait too!"

Maria inhaled sharply. "In Jonathan's living room?"

"Yes!" Elizabeth shrieked. "The man in the painting is wearing the exact same ring. With everything we've found, I'm sure we can convince the others that Jonathan is guilty."

Maria came to a stop at a red light and turned to her. "But what if we can't stop him, Elizabeth?" she asked, her eyes wide with terror.

Jessica tossed a purple tank top into the open suitcase on her bed, then turned her attention to the skirts hanging in her closet. She hadn't worn most of them in ages, which was why they were in her closet. Her favorite outfits were strewn about the floor or draped across her dresser, her chair, and every other available surface.

She noticed a corner of jade silk poking out from under a pile of blue jeans. "My new shirt," she said, pulling out the rumpled blouse. She held it up under her chin and turned to look in the mirror on her closet door.

Smoothing out the wrinkles, she debated whether to pack the jade blouse. *This would look fantastic with Liz's black pleated skirt,* Jessica thought. For a moment she considered leaving the blouse behind for her twin. But a better idea popped into her head.

Tossing the blouse into the suitcase, she rushed through the bathroom and into her sister's room. Without hesitating, she pulled open Elizabeth's closet and found the black skirt. "This really isn't her style, anyway," Jessica mumbled. She continued flipping through her twin's perfectly organized hangers, removing several more outfits that she considered not to be Elizabeth's style.

Back in her room, Jessica jammed everything into the suitcase. It was so full, she had to push down on the lid with her knee to close it.

After she'd finished packing, Jessica went back to

her sister's room for one long, last look. Just like Elizabeth, everything in the bedroom was neat and orderly. Not a single shoe, CD, magazine, or discarded wad of paper littered the floor; nothing stuck out of the drawers. Smiling, Jessica shook her head in amazement. She still couldn't understand how two girls who looked so much alike could be so different.

"Good-bye, Elizabeth," she whispered. She closed the door softly and turned to go. A tear slipped down her cheek, but she hastily brushed it away.

Jonathan, she thought, her heart pounding. A sense of urgency propelled her. It was as if she could hear his voice in her mind, calling out to her, drawing her to him. *I have to go to him now.*

Several cars were already parked in front of the Patman mansion when Maria and Elizabeth arrived. "Looks like the gang's all here," Maria remarked, tossing her keys into her bag.

Elizabeth groaned. "Somehow the word *gang* gives me a bad feeling."

"This whole situation is one big, bad feeling," Maria replied. "That's why we're here, Liz. We have to figure out a solution to this terrible mess. And the more minds together, the better, right?"

Elizabeth nodded, even though she remained doubtful. *I just hope we're not making a big mistake,* she added silently.

Miranda, the Patmans' maid, answered the door and ushered Maria and Elizabeth to the massive rec room in the basement, where everyone was gathered. Elizabeth's eyes immediately sought out Todd.

She saw him sitting on the other side of the room. He looked up, as if he'd sensed her watching him, and raised his eyebrows in silent welcome.

"We can trap the killer with a decoy," Bruce was saying. "We'll take a life-size doll, fix it up so it looks like an average kid, and leave it in a deserted part of town. Then we wait in our cars. When the murderer appears, we run him down."

"That's the most ridiculous thing I've ever heard," Lila proclaimed.

"I sort of like it," Winston Egbert said.

Lila glared at him. "You would," she snapped.

"I want to be driving the car that hits the guy," Amy growled, her gray eyes burning with grief and fury. "I want him to pay for killing my cousin."

Maria signaled for attention. "Elizabeth and I have something to tell you guys. And it's pretty . . . weird," she added.

"Can't be any weirder than what these jokers have come up with," Lila grumbled.

Elizabeth took a deep breath and began. "We're pretty sure that the killer is Jonathan."

A chorus of objections rose from the group.

Apparently everyone admired Jonathan.

"It can't be him," Ken Matthews countered. "Jonathan was upstairs with Jessica when the lights went out at the party."

Elizabeth saw a flicker of pain in Ken's blue eyes. She wondered if he still hadn't gotten over his breakup with Jessica.

Maria shook her head. "There's more. And this is where it gets strange, so brace yourselves," she warned. "We have reason to believe that Jonathan is a vampire!"

Lila let out a hoot of laughter. "And I thought Bruce was crazy!" she said. "You two are *really* insane!"

"Sounds like a fun theory, but there are no such things as vampires," Winston explained. "Most of the vampire stuff we have today comes to us from stories created during the Victorian era to replace the racy novels that had become taboo." He smiled proudly. "I did a report for English and got an A-plus on it," he added.

"Just listen with an open mind," Maria asked. She walked to the head of the pool table and placed her papers on it, as if it were a podium. "Point number one—Jonathan arrived at the same time the murders began."

"Wait a minute," Tim Nelson protested. "You can't automatically assume—"

Maria held up her hand. "I know, I know. It's all circumstantial. I said the same thing myself at first, right, Liz?" She glanced at Elizabeth for confirmation.

"I realize it sounds unbelievable," Elizabeth admitted. "But when you begin adding everything together . . . for instance, there was a series of murders in Mount Creshnor in 1938, the same year that a guy named John Cayne graduated from high school there."

Maria went on to explain what they'd found in their research about vampires. "They don't appear in photographs. Have any of you ever seen Jonathan in a photograph?" she asked pointedly.

No one answered.

"Olivia took pictures at Katrina's funeral, but Jonathan doesn't appear in any of them," Maria added. "Now, I know what you're all thinking— Jonathan comes out during the day, and vampires aren't supposed to do that."

She read the passage in her notes about vampires' talismans. "This stuff describes Jonathan perfectly. It says vampires don't generally eat solid food. Have any of you seen him eat during lunch?"

Elizabeth blinked. "I remember when he came over for Sunday dinner. He hardly ate a bite. And there's also direct evidence linking him to the recent killings," she pointed out. "Earlier this week, Jonathan took Jessica to a cave at the beach and told her it was his private hideout—and that's the same place where police have found traces of the victims' blood."

When Elizabeth and Maria were finished, the room fell silent. Everyone seemed totally astonished.

"If anyone here can explain all this in any other way, I'd love to hear it," Maria challenged.

Elizabeth looked at the bewildered faces around the room. "I know it sounds incredible," she murmured.

"But it adds up," Aaron Dallas said.

A.J. Morgan raked his hand through his red hair. "Hey, Todd, what about the time Jonathan shot baskets with us? The guy was amazing!" he exclaimed with a heavy southern drawl. A.J. had moved to Sweet Valley from Georgia and was on the varsity basketball team with Todd. "Aren't vampires supposed to have extreme physical powers?" he asked.

Maria slapped her hand on the stack of papers in front of her. "You're absolutely right! It's all in here."

Slowly the group came around, everyone adding their own evidence against Jonathan. "We have to stop him," Maria declared.

"You bet we do!" Amy shouted. "But how?"

Maria lowered her gaze and flipped through her papers. "I found an article that tells how. Some of this is terribly gruesome," she warned. "'Methods to kill the undead,'" she read aloud. "There's a whole list of ways: boiling its head in vinegar . . . chopping off its head with a gravedigger's shovel and stuffing its mouth with uncooked rice . . . driving a wooden stake through its heart—"

"The proverbial stake through the heart," Winston interjected. "It always works in the movies."

"Vampires can't cross a rushing stream," Maria continued, "so throwing it into a stream or a river would kill it, except that the vampire can fly across by changing into a bat or bird." She lowered her eyes to the page. "And fire would kill it."

"A fire!" Bruce yelled. "That's it. Let's go burn down Jonathan's house. That place is a firetrap anyway. And if Jonathan isn't home, we'll hunt him down and set him on fire too."

Elizabeth was shocked when everyone seemed to agree with Bruce's suggestion. "Wait a minute!" she cried, hoping to restore order. "We can't go around setting houses and people on fire!"

"I agree," Bruce replied. "But Jonathan Cain isn't exactly a *person*, is he?"

"That's right," Barry Rork remarked, scowling. "I can't believe I'm saying this, but your vampire theory sounds right on the mark."

Bruce clenched his teeth and exhaled sharply. "I can't believe I let that creep hang out with me."

"I want Jonathan Cain to suffer—and *die*—for killing my cousin!" Amy shouted.

"It won't bring Katrina back!" Elizabeth retorted. "Come on, guys, let's be reasonable." She looked to Maria for help, but her friend was right there with Bruce, leading the impassioned movement.

Todd stood up, raising his hands. "Elizabeth's right. Jonathan is still innocent until proven guilty."

Elizabeth swallowed hard, deeply touched by his support.

"Oh, sure," Lila snapped. "But what about Katrina? She was innocent until proven *dead!*"

Heather Mallone, the cocaptain of the Sweet Valley High cheerleading squad, began sobbing. "I'm just so sick of being afraid all the time. I can't sleep, my complexion is sallow . . . I'm a wreck! I say let's get rid of Jonathan Cain before he kills again," she wailed.

"Heather's got a good point," Ken said. "I'm sure he'll kill again if we don't act now."

"I agree we have to act," Elizabeth countered. "But let's be sensible."

Bruce shook his fist in the air. "The time for being sensible is over," he shouted. "Now it's time to wipe out the enemy. We're not going to let Jonathan Cain get away with his crimes!" Shouts of agreement clamored through the rec room.

"He messed up Enid pretty badly," Todd

remarked, glancing at Elizabeth with a look of apology. "Something has to be done."

The room shook as everyone began shouting for revenge.

"Listen to me!" Elizabeth pleaded. "Enid is my best friend." She choked back a sudden sob and drew in a deep breath. "I'm as angry as everyone else is about what Jonathan did to her and to Katrina and those other kids."

"Then why are you wimping out all of a sudden?" Maria raged at her.

"Because taking the law into our hands isn't the solution," Elizabeth shouted back.

"Why not?" Sandy Bacon retorted, tossing back her short dark-blond hair. "The law sure isn't in the *police's* hands."

Elizabeth's temper flared hotter. "Would you people get real? Instead of committing arson, let's march into the police station together with all this stuff and demand that they take action."

Maria snorted. "Yeah, right, Elizabeth. We were just there yesterday, in case you've forgotten. The detective in charge offered to put you in touch with a Japanese psychic. That's what's they think of our proof," she declared hotly. "And in the meantime, more dead bodies—*sans* hemoglobin—will be showing up around town."

Amy Sutton climbed on top of a marble coffee

table and screamed, "I want revenge!" The crowd responded with a bloodcurdling cheer.

Bruce shouted over the noise of the crowd. "Are we going to sit back and wait for the police to handle this?"

A resounding "No!" rang out through the room. Everyone began rushing toward Bruce, shoving Elizabeth against the wall.

"Are we going to let that cold-blooded monster kill again?" Bruce hollered.

"No!"

"Are we afraid to hunt him down?" he asked.

"No!"

"Will we show mercy?"

"No!" Everyone cheered and began to chant, "Kill the killer, kill the killer . . ."

Chapter 13

Elizabeth gaped in horror at the explosion of rage in Bruce's rec room. She craned her neck to catch a glimpse of Todd, but he'd disappeared into the throng. Even Winston, the one person who could usually be counted on to see the lighter side of things and to crack a joke at the most inappropriate times, seemed to be caught up in the flaming anger.

In the midst of the commotion, Elizabeth noticed Miranda standing at the door with a concerned look on her face, her gaze sweeping across the room.

Elizabeth inched her way through the crowd to see if there was something wrong. She was surprised when Miranda told her that she was wanted on the telephone.

"It's Ms. Rollins calling. She said it was urgent. You can use the extension in the room across the hall, if you prefer," Miranda offered. "It's much quieter."

A fist of panic squeezed Elizabeth's heart. She ran to the small sitting room across the hall and picked up the phone. When she tried to speak, only a pathetic, anguished cry emerged.

"Enid is going to be OK," Adele Rollins said immediately. "She's come out of the coma."

Elizabeth exhaled the breath she'd been holding and collapsed onto the leather couch. "That's wonderful!"

"Oh, yes, isn't it?" Enid's mother exclaimed. "She's downstairs in X-ray for more tests, but so far the results are positive. There's every indication that she'll have a complete recovery." Ms. Rollins's voice was thick with emotion.

"I'm so happy, and relieved," Elizabeth said, tears streaming down her face. "I don't know what I would have done if—" Her voice broke on a sob.

"I know, dear," Ms. Rollins replied. Then she asked, "Do you know where I can get in touch with Jonathan Cain?"

Elizabeth gulped. "Oh, no. Did Enid say more?"

"I'd like to get him a gift certificate from Music Center as a gesture of thanks. Even though that doesn't come close to showing how grateful I am," Ms. Rollins said.

"What?" Elizabeth gasped. "What did Enid say about Jonathan?"

"I'm sorry, I forgot to tell you. Jonathan Cain is the guy who found Enid and brought her to the emergency room Monday night," Ms. Rollins explained.

Elizabeth felt as though she'd been struck. "Are you sure it was Jonathan Cain?"

"Yes, Enid remembered it clearly. That boy saved my daughter's life," Ms. Rollins added emphatically. "Elizabeth, I have to run, but I'm glad I was able to track you down tonight. When Todd's mother told me he was at Bruce's house, I figured that's where I'd find you too. I did leave a message on your answering machine when I phoned your house, but I wanted you to hear the great news as soon as possible. I know how worried you've been."

"Thanks," Elizabeth said, her mind still reeling about Jonathan. Her hand shook as she hung up the phone.

Jonathan Cain saved Enid's life? she repeated to herself. It didn't seem possible. *Could I have totally misjudged him?* she wondered.

Elizabeth suddenly remembered the raging crowd down the hall. She had to stop them before they did something really crazy. But when she returned to the rec room, everyone was gone—including Maria, her ride. "Now what?" Elizabeth cried frantically.

Something Enid's mother had said popped into her mind. Ms. Rollins had mentioned that she'd left a message for Elizabeth on the Wakefields' answering machine. *That means Jessica wasn't home to pick up the phone!* she realized.

Hoping she was wrong, she picked up the extension in the rec room and tried calling Jessica at home. When the answering machine picked up, Elizabeth disconnected the call and immediately called information for Jonathan's number, assuming that was where her sister had gone. No one answered at his house, either.

"What am I supposed to do now?" Elizabeth shrieked. She was stranded at the Patman mansion without a ride, Jessica was in terrible danger, and a mob of vigilantes was on the loose—hunting down the guy who had saved Enid's life!

Jessica arrived at Jonathan's house and hopped out of the Jeep. A huge, full moon blazed in the dark sky, casting strange shadows everywhere. But Jessica realized she was no longer afraid of being alone in the desolate area. Jonathan's house seemed welcoming. She was drawn to it, and to him.

Jessica stood and gazed at the crumbling mansion. A gust of wind whistled through the gnarled old tree in the front yard. A loose shutter banged against the side of the house, and the front yard was overgrown with weeds. Jessica smiled tenderly, tears of joy filling her eyes. *I'm home!* she thought.

She hurried to the front door, eager to be in Jonathan's arms. As she raised her hand to the ornate brass knocker, Jonathan opened the door. "I've been waiting for you," he said.

He led her inside and kicked the door shut. "My sweet Jessica," he whispered, his breath tickling her forehead. He gazed into her eyes, and Jessica felt as if she were drowning—willingly.

"Come with me," he commanded. He took her into the living room and pointed to the portrait hanging over the fireplace. "When you said he looked just like me, you didn't know how right you were. The man in that painting wanted a better life. For a taste of luxury and the clothes of a dandy, he paid dearly."

Jessica hugged his arm. "You sound so sad."

"You have a right to know why," Jonathan replied.

He led her to a small den and turned on a dusty lamp. Jessica stood in the doorway and looked around the dimly lit room, curious and a little afraid of what she would soon learn about Jonathan.

He ran his hand along a section of the wall and a panel across the room sprang open, revealing another bookcase. "One of the good points of having an old house," he drawled. "They don't build secret panels like this anymore." He glanced at her and winked, then began looking through the secret bookcase. "And now for your answers . . ."

All of a sudden his back stiffened and his fists clenched at his sides. "Jessica, I'm afraid I'll have to leave Sweet Valley very soon," he said, his voice deadly cold.

Jessica ran to him. "What's wrong?" she asked.

He grabbed her by the shoulders and pulled her close so that their faces nearly touched. "This place isn't safe for me anymore. Someone has been here and stolen—" He took a deep, shaky breath. "Jessica, I have to go, and so should you. Go home. Now. Before it's too late."

"I won't let you go anywhere without me," Jessica cried. "No matter what you've done."

"You don't understand!" he growled.

"I don't care, Jonathan. I love you. Whatever trouble you're in, we'll face it together. I'll never leave you," she promised.

Jonathan held her tightly. "But I'm not like you, Jessica," he moaned. "We can't stay together."

Jessica leaned back and looked up at him. "You're wrong, Jonathan. We're going to be together. Forever. You're my destiny."

They gazed into each other's eyes for a long time.

"Then so be it, my love," Jonathan whispered. "*Forever.*"

"Joey, I need your help," Elizabeth pleaded, clasping the phone tightly against her ear.

"What happened to you today?" he asked. "I've been trying to reach you since this morning."

Elizabeth leaned against the edge of the pool table. "How quickly can you get to Sweet Valley?"

"Depends," he replied. "What's this all about?"

"Terrible trouble." Elizabeth wound the telephone cord around her fingers as she spoke. "I'm at Bruce Patman's house."

"What are you doing there?" Joey demanded.

"It's a long story," she said. "We met here to figure out what to do about the murders in Sweet Valley. Then everyone became convinced that Jonathan is the killer and that he's a vampire."

Joey whistled incredulously. "Wow! Who's the nut that came up with *that* theory?"

Elizabeth winced—and skipped the answer. She told him about Ms. Rollins's call and how everyone had abandoned her to seek revenge on their own. "There's a vicious mob after Jonathan, and I'm pretty sure Jessica is with him," Elizabeth sobbed. "Please hurry! I'm so afraid."

"Let me get this straight, Elizabeth. You and I supposedly had a date today, but you stood me up. Now you expect me to come running to Sweet Valley because you're worried about your sister?"

"You don't seem to understand," Elizabeth shrieked. She took a deep breath and tried to discipline her voice before she completely lost control. "This is a desperate emergency, Joey. Something horrible might happen."

"Well, it's going to have to happen without me," he responded evenly. "Now, if you were calling because you're dying to see me, or even to apologize for ditching me today . . ."

Elizabeth's blood began to boil. "This isn't the time for games, Joey. I'm begging. Either you come and help me now, or it's over between us."

"OK," he said. "If that's the way you want it, then I guess it's over."

Shaking with fury, Elizabeth slammed down the telephone receiver and cursed. She couldn't believe she'd ever considered herself in love with Joey. *I don't even* like *the jerk!* she thought, fuming.

Todd stood in the doorway of the rec room and watched Elizabeth slam down the phone. Seeing how upset she was, he was glad he hadn't taken off with the others. He'd rushed outside with everyone but turned back before he'd even started his car. Even if Elizabeth no longer cared for him, Todd couldn't get himself to leave her behind.

Now, having overheard the last bit of her telephone conversation with Joey Mason, Todd was hopeful of another chance with her. "Elizabeth?" he called softly.

She spun around and rushed into his arms. "I'm so glad you're here," she cried.

Todd swallowed hard, his heart pounding as he held her close.

"Enid woke up from her coma and said that Jonathan is the one who found her after the attack," Elizabeth explained, her words tumbling out excitedly. "*He* brought her to the hospital."

Todd paused, letting the news sink in fully. "That's great about Enid," he said. "But Jonathan? That doesn't sound like something a vampire would do. Maybe you're wrong about him."

"I don't know what to believe," Elizabeth groaned. "And when I called home, Jessica wasn't there. She's probably with Jonathan right now, but there's no answer at his house either. If Bruce, Maria, and the others find them . . ." Elizabeth's eyes widened, as if she'd just remembered something. "I have an idea where they might be," she said. "Come on, Todd, we have to find them—*fast*."

They ran out of the Patman mansion and hopped into Todd's BMW. "Where are we going?" he asked.

"To the cave where Jonathan took Jessica Monday night," Elizabeth replied as she fastened her seat belt. "Jessica said he goes there a lot."

Todd quickly started the car and turned on the headlights. "Then they're safe for a while, right?"

Elizabeth shook her head. "Maria knows where the cave is. I told her about it."

"Well, in that case—" The tires squealed as Todd whipped the BMW around and rushed out of the driveway.

In the shelter of the snug, warm cave, Jessica leaned back against Jonathan's chest. She could feel his breath, cool and soft, against her ear. His arms held her firmly. Just outside the cave, a roaring fire burned brightly. And beyond the fire, the ocean waves splashed rhythmically against the rocks, lulling her to a deep, soothing peacefulness.

Jessica sighed deeply. "I can understand why you come here, Jonathan. I feel like I'm floating on a dreamy cloud."

Jonathan brushed his lips across her ear, sending thrills all through her body. "You're the answer to my dreams, Jessica. But I don't want you to make a mistake that you'll someday regret." He shifted their positions so that they were sitting face-to-face. "Regret will eventually turn to bitterness. You would hate me, as I've come to hate—"

He stopped abruptly and drew in a harsh breath. "I want you to think carefully what it would mean for you to come with me. You would

182

be with *me,* Jessica, always—and only—with me."

She met his gaze directly. Her mind grew fuzzy, as if the dreamy clouds were moving into her brain, wiping out her ability to think. She couldn't quite grasp the meaning of his words, but her heart felt totally sure and willing to do anything he asked. "I've already told you, Jonathan. I'll never abandon you. You're my destiny."

They sat quietly, holding each other. Jessica rested her head on Jonathan's shoulder and watched the flames of their fire dancing in the dark. The full moon shone brightly over the ocean, illuminating the foamy swirls of the crashing waves. The wet rocks and sand glistened.

In a far corner of her mind, Jessica remembered lazy days spent at the beach, sunbathing, gossiping, and checking out guys with her friends. She thought of Saturday nights at the Beach Disco and cheerleading at football games. But the images grew hazy and meaningless.

Jessica sighed wistfully. She did feel a twinge of sadness at the thought of never seeing her family again, especially her twin. *But my destiny chose me the first time I saw Jonathan,* she reminded herself. Jessica couldn't imagine living without him.

Jonathan cupped her chin in his hand and looked deeply into her eyes, probing her heart with his gaze. "Will you follow me?" he whispered.

She nodded mutely. He smiled and kissed her lips gently. "Thank you, Jessica."

All of a sudden a cold, tingling sensation shot through her. Jessica realized she was trembling, her heart squeezing with terror. Her gut screamed at her to run away as fast as she could before she completely lost her sanity.

But then Jonathan tightened his arms around her, and her fears drifted away like dry flower petals in the breeze. Jessica snuggled closer to him and sighed. Willingly she let herself sink deeper into the soothing spell of Jonathan's love.

Gradually the clouds in her mind grew thicker, blotting out the memories of her past life, until Jessica could hardly picture her parents' faces anymore; she couldn't recall her brother's first name. Only Jonathan seemed real. She didn't need anyone else. Her heart, mind, and life were now his.

Jonathan clasped her hand, entwining their fingers. Jessica touched his ring with her other hand, running her fingertip along the ridges of inlaid silver and onyx. "We'll never be able to be in the sun together after this night," he said.

Jessica blinked. "I know that . . . no, wait, I don't know." She shook her head. "Jonathan, I'm so confused."

He kissed her forehead and gently pushed her

hair behind her shoulders. "It's OK, my darling. I'm here with you, as I will always be." He placed his fingers over hers on the ring. "Without this, the sun's rays would destroy me. I'll share my ring with you, but we'll have to take turns wearing it."

Jessica smiled, a warm glow radiating through her. Although she didn't grasp the meaning of what he'd said, she was satisfied with the bits she'd understood. *Jonathan is happy. He'll share his ring with me. We'll be together always,* she told herself. *And nothing else matters.*

Chapter 14

"I hope this is the right way," Elizabeth said as Todd turned onto a narrow, unmarked road. The BMW bounced along the uneven surface, setting her teeth on edge. A few minutes later they came to a dead end, the headlights illuminating a stretch of sandy beach.

Elizabeth and Todd hopped out of the car. A gust of wind came up off the ocean, whipping back Elizabeth's open jacket like a sail. "I think the cave is farther south along the shore," she said, fastening the buttons on her jacket.

Todd grabbed two flashlights from the trunk and handed one to her. "We'll just have to search until we find it," he remarked.

"Thank you, Todd," Elizabeth said softly.

A fleeting smile hovered on his lips. "For the flashlight?"

Elizabeth nodded. "And for being here for me—again."

Todd put his hand on her shoulder. "You're welcome. Now, I suggest we get going before the Sweet Valley mob beats us to that cave."

Following the beams of their flashlights, Elizabeth and Todd found a path leading away from the main beach. "I'll bet that's the way," Elizabeth said.

They followed the path as it wound through a salt marsh, ending on a narrow beach at the bottom of a rocky cliff. Elizabeth and Todd shone their flashlights along the jagged rocks. "Jonathan's cave could be anywhere around here," Elizabeth complained. "We'll never find it in the dark."

"We have to keep looking," Todd replied encouragingly.

After a few minutes Elizabeth spotted the glow of a fire some distance away. "Todd, look! Maybe it's them."

They took off running at full speed, their feet kicking up puffs of sand. Elizabeth's heart pounded—from running and from fear of what they might find. As they approached the fire they slowed their pace. Todd clasped Elizabeth's hand. "Look. I think that's it," he whispered, shining his flashlight on an opening in the rocks.

"You're right," Elizabeth gasped. She ran the

rest of the way and dropped to her knees at the entrance of the cave. Jonathan was sitting with his back against the side of the cave, his long legs stretched out before him, his booted feet crossed at the ankles. Jessica was snuggled in his arms, partly lying across his lap.

Jonathan turned to Elizabeth with a bland expression, his eyes glowing in the light of the campfire. Forcing herself to ignore him and her revulsion, Elizabeth focused on her twin. "Jessica?" she whispered breathlessly.

Jessica kept her head lowered, her face tucked into the crook of Jonathan's neck, as if she hadn't heard her name called. Elizabeth frowned, a creeping uneasiness clawing at her heart. "Are you OK?" she asked, reaching for her sister's hands. They were icy. Jessica seemed completely unaware of Elizabeth's presence.

"Look at me, Jess!" she demanded. She lifted Jessica's chin and gasped. Jessica's eyes were wide and unfocused, and her lips were twisted into a broad, eerie smile. It was the look of madness.

Elizabeth opened her mouth to speak—or to scream. Nothing came out but a wheezy, high-pitched shriek.

Just then the sound of angry shouting came from farther down the beach. Todd dropped down on the sand beside Elizabeth. "Jonathan, you have to get out of here," he warned. "Everyone is after you."

Elizabeth tore her gaze from Jessica and rose to her feet. She saw an aura of flashlights and torches a short distance away and coming closer. The mob from Sweet Valley High was heading straight for the cave, screaming bloody murder.

Todd squeezed her hand. "I'll try to hold them off for a few extra minutes," he said.

Elizabeth watched as he took off running toward the raging crowd, her whole body frozen with fear.

Jonathan's jaw stiffened as he stood on the beach, watching the crowd coming toward him. *They actually mean to kill me,* he realized. He'd never fully believed the kids from Sweet Valley High would dare come after him, considering how pathetic and gullible most of them were. *Seems I've underestimated them.*

During his stay in Sweet Valley Jonathan had been treated like royalty. Everywhere he'd gone, the pitiful creatures had fawned over him shamelessly. Girls had thrown themselves at him; guys had tried to copy his style. Everyone had fallen in love with Jonathan Cain. *Nearly everyone,* he corrected himself, glancing at Jessica's twin sister.

Jonathan's eyes narrowed as he watched the girls together. Elizabeth was trying to pull her sister out of the cave, without Jessica's cooperation.

To the average eye, the sisters might look alike, but to Jonathan, the Wakefield twins had very little in common. One of them loathed him, and the other loved him as he'd never been loved before.

Jonathan exhaled wearily. He was running out of time. The Sweet Valley crowd would arrive within minutes. Throughout history, many of his kind had been forced to flee raging mobs with fiery torches. *It seems some things never change,* he reflected.

He walked back to the cave and crouched down at the entrance. A pang of regret sliced through his heart like a sharp, cold knife. "Jessica, I have to leave immediately."

Elizabeth wedged herself between them. "Stay away from her!" she screamed.

Jonathan leaned back and gazed at her. To his surprise, she met his eyes with a look of defiance, even though she was obviously terrified. He couldn't help but admire her courage—and her love for Jessica. Reluctantly he stepped away from the cave.

Suddenly Jessica pushed her way past Elizabeth and threw herself into his arms. "Take me with you!" she pleaded.

Elizabeth jumped up and screeched, "No, Jessica!"

But Jessica held on to him tightly, her blue-green eyes shining with passion. *She's mine,* he realized. *It would be so easy to—* "No!" he cried, tearing himself away.

"Please, Jonathan!" she sobbed, running after him.

Elizabeth chased after her sister, screaming hysterically.

When he reached the edge of the surf, Jonathan stopped and turned around to face Jessica. Elizabeth had a tight grip on her sister's jacket, holding her back.

Seeing Jessica's face wet with tears and her eyes filled with anguish ripped into Jonathan's heart. Waves of despair shuddered through his body.

"I thought we were going to be together, just you and me—*forever*," she cried, reaching her arms out to him as Elizabeth tried to drag her away. "You promised you'd take me with you, Jonathan."

"I want to," he admitted, his voice trembling with pain. "But seeing the love that surrounds you, I can't bring myself to take you away."

"Please, Jonathan!" Jessica tore herself from her sister's hold and threw herself into his arms. "I can't live without you." She clutched at his shoulders, sobbing. "You told me it would be forever."

"My darling," he groaned. There was no way Jessica could understand the aching loneliness and gloom she would find in the dark life. He'd fooled himself into thinking she might be happy with him. Now he had to give her the gift that he himself had lost—to be allowed to live in the light.

"My world is one of darkness; you belong in the

sunlight." Tears pooled in Jonathan's eyes as he loosened Jessica's grip and gently pushed her away. Elizabeth immediately gathered her up in her arms.

Forcing himself to be as strong as his love, Jonathan turned and ran, the piercing sounds of Jessica's cries ringing in his ears—and shattering his heart.

Elizabeth watched as Jonathan's shadowy form seemed to disappear into the dark ocean. Jessica screamed and struggled to pull away, but Elizabeth yanked her back, both of them toppling onto the damp sand.

"Leave me alone!" Jessica shrieked. She elbowed herself out of Elizabeth's grip and jumped to her feet.

But Elizabeth was right behind her and managed to regain her hold. "You can't go with him," she yelled. "It's all over, Jess."

Jessica froze for a moment, as if she'd gone into shock. "It's over?" she whispered.

"That's right," Elizabeth said gently.

Jessica sat down on the sand and drew her knees up to her chin. "Why did he have to go away?" She sounded like a lost child.

"He just did," Elizabeth replied. She sat next to her sister and put her arm around her shoulders. "He had to go, Jess."

Jessica covered her face with her hands and

wept, her whole body shaking. Elizabeth cried too. Now that the terror had passed, a million different emotions ripped through Elizabeth in the aftershock.

Minutes later the SVH mob arrived on the spot, calling for Jonathan. Their angry faces appeared distorted and hideous in the glow of their flashlights and torches.

Elizabeth rose to her feet as Todd ran over to her. "Is everything OK?" he asked, hugging her close to his side.

She nodded, grateful for his solid presence. Together they faced the angry crowd.

"Jonathan is gone," Todd told them.

Everyone began talking at once. "We can't let him get away . . . has to pay for the killings . . . death to the killer . . . find him no matter what . . ."

Finally Bruce raised his hands, and the mob became silent. "Tell us where Jonathan went!" he demanded.

"We don't know," Elizabeth shot back.

Maria glared at her. "Why are you protecting him all of a sudden?"

"I'm not," Elizabeth snapped. She took a deep breath and exhaled wearily. "The killing is over, guys. Enid is going to be OK. Jonathan has disappeared, and Jessica is safe."

❖　　　❖　　　❖

Jessica heard her sister's words, and another wave of hot, bitter tears flooded her eyes. *He's gone,* her mind cried. But her heart refused to believe it.

All around her, people were yelling. She couldn't understand what they were saying, and she didn't care. *Why did you leave me, Jonathan?* she thought, her heart twisted in anguish.

Through her tears, she spotted a glimmer in the sand, a small object caught in the light of the full moon. Jessica held her breath as she moved toward it.

Just as she'd known in her heart, it was Jonathan's ring. Her hand trembled as she picked it up and held it in her open palm. It felt warm, as if it were alive. Jessica admired the ornate pattern of silver and onyx around the wooden circumference. The first time she'd noticed it on Jonathan's hand, she'd vowed that he would give it to her someday.

Jessica kissed the ring and slipped it on her finger. It was much too large, so she closed her hand to hold it secure. It was all she had left of him now. She resolved to wear it on a chain around her neck and treasure it always.

Tears streamed down Jessica's face. *I never imagined that I'd get Jonathan's ring but lose him,* she thought sadly.

A huge black crow rose from the Pacific Ocean

and flew toward her. Jessica watched as the bird circled above her head, dipped a wing, then disappeared into the dark night. "Good-bye, Jonathan," Jessica whispered. "I'll love you forever."

A short distance away, Todd and Elizabeth stood together in the moonlight. The crowd had dispersed, and now Elizabeth was left with her own mess to resolve.

She looked out toward the ocean. There was so much she wanted to say to Todd. She still loved him, but she couldn't find the words to tell him.

She needed to make him understand how deeply she regretted her recent lies and deception about Joey. *I've treated Todd so badly,* she admitted to herself. *Will he ever be able to forgive me and give me another chance?*

But when Elizabeth turned to him, she saw the answer in the dark pools of Todd's warm brown eyes. Her breath caught in her throat as he gently pulled her into his arms. As their lips met in a glorious, passionate kiss, Elizabeth realized that words weren't necessary.

Enid woke up in a cold sweat, her whole body shivering. *Something's wrong,* she thought.

She sat up and looked around for whatever had startled her. With the light of the full moon shining into her hospital room, she could make out the shapes of the flowers and gifts that adorned every available surface. A bunch of shiny balloons hovered over the foot of her bed, tethered to the side railing.

From the corner of her eye, Enid caught a glimpse of something flickering in the window. She turned just in time to see a large dark bird perched on the ledge outside her room. In the next instant the bird took flight, disappearing into the moonlit night.

A terrible feeling of loss and anguish came over Enid, as if a piece of her heart had been torn away. Without fully understanding why, she burst into tears.

Jessica leaned back in the sand, her elbows supporting her as she stared at the shimmering ocean. Everything that had happened to her over the past few weeks seemed strange and unreal. But the sound of the crashing waves seemed to be pulling her out of a fog, waking her from a long dream. A few coherent thoughts began to emerge.

It all started the night I lost my diamond earring at the Dairi Burger, she recalled, trying to put her thoughts in order. *I rescued Jasmine from the tree in the back parking lot—and discovered a dead body in the Dumpster.* A few weeks later she had found her beloved kitten dead in the backyard. Jasmine's little body had been drained of blood.

Jessica shook her head to clear it. So many

weird, horrible things had happened all around her. *Will any of this ever make sense?* she wondered.

The sky had lightened to a shade of deep blue when Elizabeth came over and sat down beside her. "Are you OK, Jess?" she asked.

Jessica sat up and brushed the sand off her elbows. "I'm not sure," she answered truthfully. Elizabeth hugged her, and Jessica realized how much she appreciated her twin's support. *How could I have considered giving up my sister—and my whole life—for a guy?* Jessica wondered incredulously. *What happened to me?*

"It's late," Elizabeth whispered. "We should go home."

Jessica nodded absently. "I think you were right about Jonathan," she admitted. "But he wasn't completely evil. There was some good in him."

"We'll never know the whole truth," Elizabeth replied. "But at least he didn't take you away from me."

Jessica sighed. "There was something very sad about him, as if he hated himself."

"A person like that can be very dangerous," Elizabeth remarked. "It's hard to love others if you hate yourself."

"But he loved me!" Jessica protested.

"Maybe he did," Elizabeth murmured. "But I'm glad you're still here with me."

"I am too," Jessica replied. The twins hugged each other tightly, then Elizabeth rejoined Todd by the water's edge, leaving Jessica alone with her thoughts.

The clouds in the sky were tinted with shades of deep rose in the early dawn light. The mournful calls of seagulls sounded in the distance.

Jonathan did love me, Jessica reasoned. *Why else would he have left me his ring?*

As if to prove the point to herself, she glanced down at her hand. The ring was gone.

Jessica gasped and jumped to her feet. Frantically she checked the surrounding ground, sifting the sand through her fingers. She couldn't find it anywhere. The ring had disappeared.

Then Jessica looked down at her hand again. The area at the base of her finger where the ring had been was red and blistered . . . and as painful as her heart.

Discover the sweeping, romantic history of the men and women who made Lila Fowler who she is today! Don't miss the enthralling stories of Lila's ancestors in the newest Sweet Valley Saga, **The Fowlers of Sweet Valley.**

Bantam Books in the Sweet Valley High series
Ask your bookseller for the books you have missed

SIGN UP FOR THE
SWEET VALLEY HIGH®
FAN CLUB!

Hey, girls! Get all the gossip on Sweet Valley High's® most popular teenagers when you join our fantastic Fan Club! As a member, you'll get all of this really cool stuff:

- Membership Card with your own personal Fan Club ID number
- A Sweet Valley High® Secret Treasure Box
- Sweet Valley High® Stationery
- Official Fan Club Pencil (for secret note writing!)
- Three Bookmarks
- A "Members Only" Door Hanger
- Two Skeins of J. & P. Coats® Embroidery Floss with flower barrette instruction leaflet
- Two editions of *The Oracle* newsletter
- Plus exclusive Sweet Valley High® product offers, special savings, contests, and much more!

Be the first to find out what Jessica & Elizabeth Wakefield are up to by joining the Sweet Valley High® Fan Club for the one-year membership fee of only $6.25 each for U.S. residents, $8.25 for Canadian residents (U.S. currency). Includes shipping & handling.

Send a check or money order (do not send cash) made payable to "Sweet Valley High® Fan Club" along with this form to:

SWEET VALLEY HIGH® FAN CLUB, BOX 3919-B, SCHAUMBURG, IL 60168-3919

NAME_____
                        (Please print clearly)

ADDRESS_____

CITY_____ STATE _____ ZIP_____
                                                    (Required)

AGE_____ BIRTHDAY_____ / _____ / _____

Offer good while supplies last. Allow 6-8 weeks after check clearance for delivery. Addresses without ZIP codes cannot be honored. Offer good in USA & Canada only. Void where prohibited by law.
©1993 by Francine Pascal   LCI-1383-123